A Great Basin buckaroo once told me what it takes to be a cowgirl.

"A lot of heart and a bunch of skill—without the heart, you can't get the skill."

Great editors seem to meet the same qualifications, so this book is dedicated to Amanda Maciel, amazing editor and honorary cowgirl.

Read all the books about the

Phantom Stallion

෨ 1 ෨

THE WILD ONE

෨ 2 ෨

MUSTANG MOON

෨ 3 ෨

DARK SUNSHINE

෨ 4 ෨

THE RENEGADE

෨ 5 ෨

FREE AGAIN

෨ 6 ෨

THE CHALLENGER

෨ 7 ෨

DESERT DANCER

෨ 8 ෨

GOLDEN GHOST

ᵒᵒ 9 ᵒᵒ

GIFT HORSE

ᵒᵒ 10 ᵒᵒ

RED FEATHER FILLY

ᵒᵒ 11 ᵒᵒ

UNTAMED

ᵒᵒ 12 ᵒᵒ

RAIN DANCE

ᵒᵒ 13 ᵒᵒ

HEARTBREAK BRONCO

ᵒᵒ 14 ᵒᵒ

MOONRISE

ᵒᵒ 15 ᵒᵒ

THE KIDNAPPED COLT

ᵒᵒ 16 ᵒᵒ

THE WILDEST HEART

ᵒᵒ 17 ᵒᵒ

MOUNTAIN MARE

Phantom Stallion

∽ 17 ∽
Mountain Mare

TERRI FARLEY

AVON BOOKS

An Imprint of HarperCollins*Publishers*

Library of Congress Catalog Card Number:
2004099835
ISBN-10: 0-06-075845-7
ISBN-13: 978-0-06-075845-5

First Avon edition, 2005

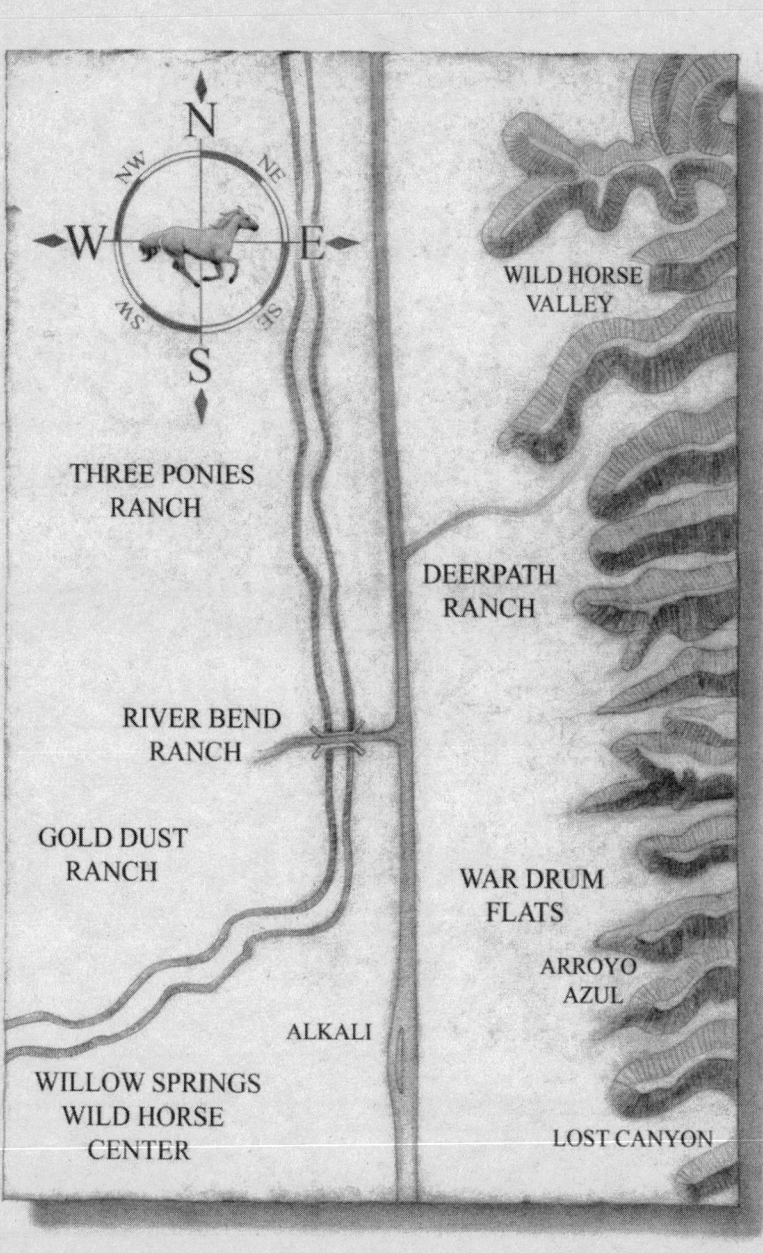

Chapter One ❧

"Look out!" Samantha Forster jerked her knees away from the gearshift as Jake jammed the truck into a lower gear and it labored uphill.

"Sorry," Jake mumbled.

Sam could tell he didn't think the bump warranted an apology.

The lurch had jolted Sam out of a restless doze. Sandwiched between her two best friends, Jake Ely and Jennifer Kenworthy, Sam should have felt cozy as they drove through the predawn darkness.

Instead, she felt cramped. She couldn't wait to escape the truck's crowded cab, saddle her horse Ace, who rode in the trailer hooked up behind the truck, and ride out into the summer morning.

Sam couldn't imagine a better saddle horse than Ace. Since she'd returned to the ranch last year, the little bay mustang had been her friend as much as the humans sitting beside her. She couldn't bear the thought of losing him, so she pushed that thought aside.

The road up to the Pinion Pine campsite was paved, but twisty and pocked with potholes. They'd lost radio reception just after starting up into the mountains. Minutes after that, Jen had fallen asleep.

Conversation would have made the drive more interesting, but Jake Ely rarely had much to say. This morning was no different.

Sam couldn't get a good look at Jake's expression. Her sideways glance caught the dull sheen of black hair tied back with a leather thong, a set jaw, and high cheekbones that showed his Shoshone heritage.

When Jake noticed her looking, he said, "Watch my hat," without taking his eyes from the road ahead.

Although Sam's and Jen's hats were on a shelf in the horse trailer, Jake's black Stetson rode on Sam's lap in the cab of the denim-blue truck.

She didn't mind. At least not much. Jake was a good friend, despite his silence. He didn't say much more to her than Ace did.

Sam drew a deep breath. If she let him read the letter she'd jammed in her pocket, Jake would give her sensible advice. But that was the last thing she wanted.

"I still say you should go with us," Sam said, returning to an earlier, safer topic.

Jake gave a grunt. It must be a sign of how long they'd known each other that Sam was able to interpret the sound to mean, *You* would *think that*.

"It'll be fun riding through the mountains, and the cattle are practically tame," she added.

Jake gave a slight shake of his head. He knew she was right, but he didn't care.

"It's your loss," she said.

She'd never ridden on the annual Darton Rodeo cattle drive and she was excited to join it today. For three days, steers and calves that would be ridden or roped during the rodeo were herded over the range and through the mountains to reach the Darton County fairgrounds. Anyone — from local businessmen and -women to tourists — could pay to experience an improved version of the Old West. Along with the dust and lowing of cattle, guest riders had luxuries cowboys didn't. Sam had heard there would be portable showers and toilets, plus an air-conditioned van for those too saddle sore to swing back onto their dude-proof horses.

"Dad promised we'd be working the cattle, not wrangling dudes," Sam reminded Jake.

During his high school rodeo days, Dad had been pals with Hal "Ride 'Em" Ryden. While Dad had turned to college, then ranching, Hal Ryden had become a famous bull rider.

Dad insisted that Hal used to come by the ranch whenever he had a rodeo within driving distance, but Sam didn't remember him. Now Hal had retired from riding, but not rodeoing. He was a successful stock contractor, supplying cattle and horses to rodeos all over the West.

He'd told Dad he enjoyed driving the stock into town the old way, but he'd taken one look at the terrain for the last day of the drive and known he'd lose some cattle if he didn't have riders who knew this range.

The last twelve miles were the most difficult, and he'd admitted he needed more help to deliver the cattle to their destination.

Although Dad couldn't spare Ross and Pepper, his cowboys, he'd asked Jake and Sam if they'd like to earn a few dollars escorting cattle down from the mountains and through a few city streets to the fairgrounds. At first, they'd both agreed.

"Did you hear that?" Jake said suddenly, interrupting Sam's thoughts. "Like a siren?" He rolled his window open an inch.

"I didn't hear anything," Sam told him. "You're just trying to distract me."

"Nope," Jake said, closing the window. "You were sayin' how the plan was 'no messin' with dudes.'"

He sounded casual, but Sam noticed the stiff set of Jake's shoulders and knew why. Jake avoided Linc

Slocum whenever he could. And Linc was playing cowboy on this rodeo cattle drive.

Linc Slocum had been looking for ways to prove himself a Westerner since he had moved to northern Nevada. Wearing expensive hats and boots, slinging around lame cowboy slang, and learning to ride didn't help. Neither did collecting exotic horses, cattle, and even bison, or bankrolling the capture of the Phantom, a stallion legendary for his ability to elude capture.

"You can't blame the rodeo commission for being grateful that Linc donated thousands of dollars for a huge fireworks display at the end of the rodeo performances," Sam said, though the words nearly stuck in her throat.

According to her stepmother, Brynna, the rodeo commission had thanked Linc Slocum by giving him a VIP pass to all rodeo events, including the cattle drive.

"Some folks got no problem seein' their money go up in smoke," Jake said, steering around a rock in the road so he wouldn't jostle the horses riding in the trailer.

Jake was right. As one of the richest men in northern Nevada, Linc didn't mind spending money on his image. This time it had worked.

Sam stifled a groan. With the trouble she had on her mind, Linc Slocum would be tough to take. Linc already considered himself a Very Important Person. Now, he'd have a pass that proved it.

They might as well have crowned him, Sam thought.

"I can take a day of his bragging and showing off if it means Ace and I have fun," Sam told Jake.

He couldn't know she was hinting at something serious.

"Lucky thing your HARP girls fell through, then," Jake said.

"Yes and no," Sam said.

HARP, the Horse and Rider Protection program, matched at-risk girls with troubled mustangs. Hosting the girls and teaching them to ride was one way River Bend Ranch made money.

But the two girls who'd been scheduled for this week's HARP program had arrived at their last counseling session with drugs in their suitcases. They'd immediately been kicked out of the program and sent to a standard juvenile facility.

The money that River Bend had counted on was lost.

Unless, Sam thought, she stepped up and put the ranch first, like Dad was always telling her she should.

At least she'd make today's wages. That was better than nothing.

Sam shifted in the cramped space between her friends. It was getting stuffy in here.

They all wore boots and jeans. Jake's tailored shirt looked like he'd ironed it before picking them up at four A.M., but she and Jen had layered flannels over T-shirts. No wonder she was hot and Jake wasn't.

Not that Jake would show it if he were uncomfortable, Sam thought. Cowboys kept quiet.

Suddenly a jolt of indignation shot through Sam. She couldn't be strong and silent about something this important.

"I got an offer for Ace," she blurted.

Sam shifted to face Jake. She saw his throat move with a swallow and heard a wisp of sound that might have been a word, but she couldn't tell what it was.

Then, sounding lazy, he asked, "Offer for Ace to—?"

"To nothing," Sam snapped. Then she lowered her voice, trying not to wake Jen. "An offer to *buy* him, Jake. For three thousand dollars."

Jake gave a low whistle.

"What's that supposed to mean?" Sam hissed.

"It's a lot of money. You sure you heard right?" He wasn't joking. Jake was being serious, boots-on-the-ground Jake.

"I've got it in writing," Sam said. She heard her own defensive tone, even as she hoped Jake was right. Maybe the extra zero was a smudge. Or a typo. But she knew it wasn't. "I got a letter from Amelia's grandmother," Sam told him.

"The snakebite kid," Jake said.

A HARP girl named Amelia had tried to keep another girl from tormenting a snake a few weeks ago. Ironically, the snake's rescuer had been the one it had bitten.

"Right. Her grandmother's on a charity board that wants to donate a therapy horse to a program for disabled kids. Amelia told her grandmother all about Ace and she thinks he'd be perfect."

Jake gave a slow nod.

Why did he have to agree? Why didn't he stare at her bug-eyed and shout that it was the most ridiculous idea he'd ever heard?

Sam knew why. Jake came from a ranch family, too. Four of his five brothers worked on the ranch. His mother turned into the ranch manager each night when she returned home after teaching history at the high school. Each morning, Jake's dad worked three hours on the range before driving to his mining office in Darton. The Three Ponies Ranch, struggling like most independent cattle operations, was at the center of the Elys' lives.

Still, Sam knew she might not have assumed she *should* sell Ace, if Dad hadn't set an example by selling his own horse, Banjo, to help River Bend Ranch. Since then, he'd ridden Jeepers-Creepers and Strawberry. Both were good working horses, full of cow sense, but neither cow pony was close to his heart like Banjo had been.

But River Bend came first, and it might be her turn to prove she understood.

She wished Jake would say something to contradict her dark thoughts. Something like, *Don't be foolish. Wyatt won't have you selling Ace.*

But she didn't see or hear a sign that Jake wanted to help her.

Sam pushed her sleeves up. It was way too hot in the truck's cab. She needed fresh air and a spicy whiff of sagebrush. Now.

If Sam hadn't been leaning past a sleeping Jen to open the passenger-side window, Jake's elbow would have jabbed her as he suddenly cranked the steering wheel to the right.

The truck bounced off the paved road.

"This's the turnoff," he explained.

"How did you see that?" Sam asked, but Jake looked up into the rearview mirror, focusing on the trailer behind them, judging the horses' reaction to the quick change of direction.

It was a good thing Jake had spotted the dirt trail that led to the campsite, because she sure hadn't.

"Did something happen?" Jen mumbled as she pushed one blond braid away from her face.

"We're here," Sam said.

"Good." Jen sat up, straightened her glasses, and sniffed. "That means I wasn't dreaming that I smelled breakfast."

Sam caught the aroma of coffee and frying ham just as she spotted a campfire blazing near a haphazard cluster of tents.

"I'll help you unload the horses," Jake said.

And then I'm outta here, his tone implied. Maybe she shouldn't have told him, Sam thought. She could have just kept the letter's contents to herself. Except that Amelia's grandmother had written that she would be phoning soon.

As Jake slowly drove the truck into camp, Sam thought the blue, green, and white tents looked like giant flowers in the mountain meadow. There were more people here than she would have guessed.

Suddenly shyness pushed aside Sam's worry.

What was she supposed to do now? Just loop her arm through Jen's, bounce into camp, and announce that the real cowgirls had arrived?

She wasn't quite that sure of herself.

Jake braked to a stop at the edge of the encampment. In the instant before he clicked off the truck's headlights, Sam saw people crawling out of their tents. Others wandered sleepily through the darkness, stretching before they lined up outside a portable toilet. A few stood around the campfire, cradling mugs and staring into the flames.

When the headlights clicked off, Sam realized she didn't know anyone here except Linc Slocum.

"Will you recognize Mr. Ryden?" Jen asked as she opened the truck door.

"Dad said I couldn't miss his hat," Sam said. "It's supposed to be an old black sombrero with a floppy brim."

She looked down at Jake's Stetson and smiled. Her spirits lifted higher than they'd been all morning. Cowboys had this *thing* for their hats.

Jen slipped from the truck and Sam scooted after her, then hopped down. Both of them looked up at a navy blue sky that was still pricked with stars.

Jake took his Stetson from Sam, pulled it on, and settled it. He blew through his lips and shook his head.

Here it comes, Sam thought. Jake had been mulling it over, in slow cowboy fashion, and he was about to tell her she had to sell Ace. For the good of River Bend Ranch. For the good of her family.

But Jake just walked on by and unlatched the back of the horse trailer.

"Never looked at a rodeo program before, huh?" he mumbled.

What was he talking about?

If Jen knew, or heard, she cared more about beating Jake into the trailer.

"Silly, good girl," Jen said as she edged between Ace and her palomino mare, Silk Stockings. "Stay put, girl," she crooned.

The palomino's white tail switched and her legs danced with eagerness. She wanted to back out of the trailer too fast, and that could be dangerous.

Jen stood beside Silly, kneading her withers for a full minute, before she jerked loose the quick-release knot. Finally, she let her horse back slowly from the trailer.

Only then did Jen stare across the mare's snowy mane at Jake.

"Now, regarding your comments about us never reading a rodeo program?" Jen said in a tone that sounded more like a college professor than a half-awake teenager. "I've seen photos of Ride 'Em Ryden. And I know he and all his pickup men ride matched black horses, too, but I don't see their saddle herd." Jen gestured toward the camp. "Besides, all horses look black in the dark."

Not all, Sam thought automatically. She knew a silver stallion that glimmered in the dark. Moonbeams flashed from his coat and sparked from his pewter hooves. Even in midnight blackness, he didn't look like other horses. The Phantom was the most beautiful animal on earth, and once he'd been hers.

But Ace was hers now.

Worry gnawed on Sam's nerves as anxiety for Ace spilled over to the Phantom.

Quit it, she told herself. She just hadn't had enough sleep.

Sam studied the mountains rising like blue-black camel's humps against the dark sky. Her grasp of local geography wasn't perfect, but she thought the Pinion Pine camp was above Lost Canyon. That wasn't exactly part of the Phantom's summer territory, but the Calico Mountains were honeycombed with trails and passages known only to wildlife.

She couldn't imagine the Phantom venturing near

the scents and sounds of a big cattle drive. But he'd surprised her before, especially when he was trying to gather new mares for his herd.

But all the mares on this drive would have riders, right?

"—makes you think his pickup men would be wranglin' dudes?" Jake muttered.

Sam smiled, distracted by her best friends' sparring. They were too much alike, both experts eager to contradict the other.

Jake entered the trailer, released Ace, and backed him out while she was still just standing there.

Sam pretended she'd been thinking about Jake's question.

"I'm not even sure what a pickup man is," she admitted.

"Good thing I was askin' Ace," Jake said as the bay gelding stopped in front of Sam and swung his head around to nuzzle her pocket.

Sam closed her eyes and reveled in the flutter of the gelding's velvety lips and the alfalfa smell of him.

Forget it, she thought. *Ace is mine 'til the end.*

"Pickup men are cowboys who work the rough-stock events, like bronc riding," Jen explained. "They rescue rodeo cowboys off the horses and release the flank straps—"

"Oh, right," Sam said. She took Ace's lead rope from Jake.

"There's more to a pickup rider's job than that,"

Jake said as he slammed the trailer doors and shot the latch into place. Then he turned to Sam. "Think you can handle things from here on out?"

"What about—?" Sam began, but then she stopped.

Even in the faint light and the shadow of his hat brim, she sensed Jake's brotherly look. It wasn't authority, exactly; it was more an attitude that said he'd probably need to bail her out and he was up to the challenge.

Sam glanced at the shadows moving around the camp. As the sky got a little lighter, there were more of them. She wished her childhood memory would kick in and she'd spot Hal Ryden, but she said, "Of course I can handle it."

"And then there's Ace," Jen joked as she pointed at the bay.

Ace's black-edged ears pricked toward the faint moos of penned cattle.

"He can handle it all without us," Sam laughed, but her faith in the horse felt bittersweet.

The jangle of an old-fashioned triangle and a call to "Come and get it" made Silly snort and spook.

If Ace were more like Silly, Sam thought, she wouldn't have this problem. No one would buy the jumpy palomino to work with disabled children.

Seeing Jen distracted, Jake touched Sam's arm.

She turned immediately, trying to analyze his expression. A campfire highlighted the shelf of his cheekbones, but left his eyes in shadow.

"Nothin's gonna happen 'til you get down off this mountain," he said. "We'll—"

Jake made a vague gesture.

"'Talk later'?" Sam asked with a laugh. "'Have a discussion'? That's what people call it, you know. And they do it all the time."

Jake ignored her teasing.

"*Adios,*" he said, then climbed into his truck and drove away with the horse trailer rattling along behind.

Jen was soothing Silly and gazing after the trailer's red taillights when Sam turned to look at the camp and saw two figures materialize out of the darkness.

"Samantha Anne Forster!" The voice boomed from the taller man. Sam couldn't see his face, but he wore a floppy, oversized hat that should have looked ridiculous, but somehow didn't. "Lord almighty, girl! You've grown up, but I'd recognize you anywhere!"

Beside him, looking pumpkin-shaped by comparison, the second man grunted, "And darned if she ain't welcome as a bedroll fulla rattlers."

Chapter Two ⧽

𝒜ce planted all four hooves. Even when Sam tugged for him to follow, he resisted her approach toward Hal Ryden and Linc Slocum.

"C'mon, boy," Sam said.

Had the little mustang turned stubborn? Maybe he'd make a terrible therapy horse after all.

But Sam knew that wasn't true. His refusal to move showed his brains. Ace had learned that chaos cropped up when he was near Linc Slocum.

Sam reached her other hand up the reins to exert pressure closer to his bit. "I don't blame you," Sam whispered to her horse. "But, c'mon."

"Now the herd'll get through for sure," Hal Ryden said, and though he was joking, Sam heard a real welcome in his words. "I can't tell you how glad I am to have you here to help." His smile took in both girls.

Apparently he hadn't heard Linc's remark about her, Sam thought. When Ace finally lifted a front hoof as if it were heavy as an anvil, then followed her with grudging steps, Sam took a better look at the man who'd been Dad's boyhood pal.

Hal Ryden stood at least six feet tall. He wore a black Western shirt with tiny teal-colored script that read RYDEN RODEO CO., but everything about him said he was a real cowboy.

His walk gave him away.

Sam couldn't explain how Hal Ryden could stride with loose-jointed grace *and* hard-hammered stiffness, but Dad moved the same way. So did Jen's dad. That buckaroo's gait came from thousands of hours in the saddle and a few being thrown from it.

Hal Ryden had the broad shoulders and raspy voice of Gram's favorite actor, John Wayne, but the warmth in his manner, as he led them closer to camp, was all his own.

"Samantha, honey, step over here closer to the fire so I can get a better look at you." Hal Ryden didn't add another word, but he hesitated.

Had he been about to say she looked just like her mother?

Instead, he touched Ace's neck with admiration.

"Nice-lookin' pony, from what I can see. Got a mind of his own. Clever, is he?"

Sam glowed at the compliment. Hal Ryden's job was handling horses and cattle, and even *he* thought Ace looked smart.

"Way too clever," Sam said, liking the man already. Then she realized she hadn't introduced Jen yet. "And so's my friend—"

Hal Ryden's laugh interrupted. "You'll have to excuse me," he said, patting Jen's shoulder. "Askin' after a horse before a young lady? That's unforgivable."

"Not at all," Jen said politely.

Sam could see Jen's manners were switched on high, despite the hour and where they were. Jen's respect for Hal "Ride 'Em" Ryden showed in the reverent way in which she extended her hand to shake his.

"I'm Jennifer Kenworthy, and I'm pleased to meet you."

"Jennifer's dad is my foreman." Sam had almost forgotten Linc was there until he cut in.

"Jed Kenworthy is a good man," Linc continued. "Jennifer here is a dandy little rider, too, and that palomino is full of cow sense, even though she's a little skittish. I'm sure they'll both do the Gold Dust Ranch proud."

Sam actually blinked in surprise. Linc Slocum's compliments were so rare, she felt suspicious. That might not be fair, but when Jen met her eyes, Sam knew she'd had the same reaction.

"I'm sure they will," Hal said. "Now, why don't you go on and get yourself some breakfast, then saddle up, Linc?"

"Well. . . ," Linc said, hesitating.

"You go on, now. I need to talk business with my new hands."

Looking as if he felt a little left out, Linc gave his belt a determined lift. The silver buckle pressed a fist-sized dent in his belly. He cleared his throat.

When the rodeo contractor showed no sign of changing his mind, Linc made the best of his banishment.

"Thanks, Hal," he said. "Your crew serves up some fine meals." He sniffed the air. "Yessir, I plan to eat so much of that maple-smoked bacon, you'll be wantin' to check me for a curly little tail."

Hal Ryden stared after Linc Slocum, then bumped back the brim of his hat.

"Ladies, you know that man. Where *does* he get those sayin's of his?"

Sam shrugged. "I know why, but I never thought about where," she said, and looked to Jen.

"It's mystifying," Jen said. "I'd guess he got them from old Western novels. You know, like Zane Grey? But he's never given any indication that he reads."

"I'm not criticizing," Hal said. "Wouldn't be any

cattle drives like this, or maybe even rodeos, if folks didn't long for the Western way of life. Then I'd have to get a desk job."

He shook his head and gazed toward the graying horizon.

"Now, as it concerns you two, Wyatt tells me you can handle a herd of range-wild cattle on your own, so this corral-bred bunch should be simple."

Jen gave a quick laugh. "How big a herd?"

"We only have a hundred head—"

Sam sucked in a breath. She and Jen had handled a herd of six grown cattle and four calves. They had been wild enough to elude capture on earlier roundups, but still, ten was a lot different than one hundred.

"—rest of the stock was trucked to the fairgrounds, so this drive is just for fun. We'll get the tricky part done by early afternoon. I have some seasoned riders along who'll keep the dudes out of your way," Hal assured them. "Dudes think they're helping, but mainly they're just harassin' those cows."

Glad for the darkness, Sam felt a blush heat her cheeks. Only last year, she'd been the one "harassin'" the cattle. Not only that, she'd actually caused a stampede.

"It's taken Ace all year to teach me to just hang on and let him do his job," she admitted.

"That's the sign of a good workin' horse—lettin'

you stay aboard until he shows you what he can do," Hal said.

"Mr. Ryden?" Jen asked, clearly thinking of something besides Ace. "After we get down off the mountains, are we taking them along the highway?" Jen asked. Her head was tilted to one side as if she were picturing the approach to Darton.

"For a little bit," Hal said. "But mostly we'll use side streets. The Sheriff's Department has put up barriers and roadblocks, and they offered help with crowd control if we need it."

Sam imagined a parade route with cheering crowds on each side as cattle stampeded down the street.

"Now, since we'll be taking them right into the fairgrounds and it's not every day someone brings a herd through town, we need to do something about your duds."

Sam didn't follow his logic, and neither did Jen.

"Duds?" Jen looked down at her jeans and the pink-and-green plaid flannel she wore over a brighter pink T-shirt.

The outfit was very subdued for Jen, Sam thought, and her own clothes were practically monochromatic.

"Isn't this okay?" Sam asked, considering her blue shirt and blue jeans.

"Didn't you two ever play dress-up?" Hal asked, grinning. "We have lots of extra duds for the rodeo grand entry—you know, at the very beginning? When we wear matching gear, it makes quite a splash."

"But, if we're really working today . . . ," Sam began carefully.

"I won't put you in anything that'll slow you down," Hal said. "Y'see, ladies, we're goin' for the look you'd wear in a Western Pleasure class at a horse show. Nothing too fancy. Real cowboy gear— chaps, gloves, vests, and such—with a touch of color. Black and blue-green are my trademark colors, mostly because they look good on any horse."

Sam hadn't thought about using color to complement a horse's coat for a long time, but suddenly she thought of the soft halter she'd fashioned for Blackie from a red flannel nightgown.

Sam smiled at the memory. The scarlet noseband and cheek pieces had framed his dark eyes and set off his ebony coat and inky mane, making him look magical. The Phantom had been an incredible horse, even as a yearling.

She blinked herself back to the present. Black and teal would look great against Ace's bay coat and Silly's palomino one, but . . .

"Not to be nosy, but since we're not in the arena—" Jen began as delicately as Sam had.

"Why do you care what we wear?" Sam finished.

"I want you girls riding point—right up front, you

know? — when we bring the herd into town. With any luck at all, you and your ponies will make the six o'clock news *and* the front page of the paper!"

Fifteen minutes later, Ace and Silly were tied to a Ryden Rodeo Productions trailer while Sam and Jen ate breakfast.

"You'll need it," Hal Ryden had said.

So they sat side by side on a log bench. They wore black fringed chaps and matching vests over blue-green shirts. Their gloves were the same lightweight black leather, styled like gauntlets, with more fringe from wrist to mid-forearm. The girls had taken them off while they ate.

"I don't know whether this is cool or embarrassing," Jen said quietly.

"Me either," Sam said.

They kept their eyes on their tin plates of biscuits covered with ham gravy, and sipped cups of orange juice.

The modern chuck wagon's sideboard had offered sausage, bacon, hash brown potatoes, and eggs every way you could imagine — scrambled, fried, ranchero-sauced, and baked in a cast-iron quiche pan with Swiss cheese. But Sam and Jen had settled for something quick.

"Maybe no one's staring at us," Sam suggested, making sure she didn't drop a blob of gravy on the expensive chaps.

"You think I'm going to look up and check?" Jen answered.

They listened as snips of conversation swirled around them. Voices wondered if the last day's terrain was as challenging as rumored, if their backs would hold out, if someone would take photographs, and if real cowgirls always kept to themselves.

Hearing that, Jen's fork paused at the same time as Sam's.

"I guess these outfits really aren't too fancy," Sam said, and Jen understood instantly.

"That's what I was thinking," Jen responded. "They'd think we're entertainers of some sort, if we looked that flashy."

"Celebrity cowpokes," Sam teased as Jen sipped her juice.

Jen's short laugh and muttered "Yeah, right," made her cough as she swallowed. She shook her head and added, "I don't think we'll be too hot, either. Hal Ryden's a real cowboy at heart. I don't think he'd handicap us just for looks."

Sam nodded as her mind veered back to meeting Hal Ryden.

"Do you think he heard what Linc said about me? Like, how unhappy he was to see me here?" Sam asked.

"If he did, he probably thought Linc was joking," Jen said.

"You know, I have plenty of reasons not to like

Linc Slocum," Sam said, "but why does he hate me?"

"Do you want those reasons in alphabetical, chronological, or random order?" Jen joked.

"No, really," Sam said, glancing up to see Linc drinking coffee with a knot of other riders. "What did I do?"

Jen drew a deep breath, as if this recitation would take plenty of oxygen.

"Provided information that prevented him from adopting the Phantom, took a photo that kept him from forcing BLM to capture the Phantom after he offered that reward for the stallion that stole Hotspot," Jen went on, counting on fingers that sprung out from holding her plate. "You uncovered his skulduggery with Karla Starr and the whole Brahma bull scheme—"

"Okay, okay," Sam said as Jen prepared to continue.

"Definitely not okay," Jen contradicted her. "Every time you turn around, you find him making a fool of himself."

"How is that my fault?"

"It's not," Jen said, then she elbowed Sam and nodded toward Slocum. "But he's probably afraid you'll tell his new friends about it and give him away."

Sam lifted her eyelashes enough to see that Linc was trying to be one of the gang with Duke Fairchild, Katie Sterling, Hal Ryden, and some other people she didn't recognize. The ones Sam could see from where she sat were all smiling politely, but she'd bet they weren't taken in by Linc Slocum's forced friendliness.

"He's almost pitiful, isn't he?" Jen said as she watched.

"No, not after what he did to the Phantom," Sam said.

As long as the stallion wore the scar Linc had inflicted, she couldn't feel sorry for the man. Besides that, Sam couldn't help being jealous. She should probably sell Ace to benefit those she loved. Linc Slocum was so rich, he never did without anything he wanted.

Just then, a woman moved away from the group. Hal Ryden walked with her, and Linc Slocum tagged along.

Sam and Jen stood up as they approached, and even though Hal lowered his voice, Sam heard him warn Linc. "That was a right colorful expression, about the bedroll full of rattlers, but Samantha's the daughter of one of my oldest friends and I surely do hope you were jokin'."

Before Sam's mind processed what her ears had overheard, a friendly voice interrupted.

"Samantha Foster, isn't it?"

The fresh-faced woman who'd walked over with Hal wore a red bandanna neatly knotted over a white shirt. Her blond hair looked stylishly windblown and Sam was pretty sure she was wearing makeup despite the time and place.

"Sam *Forster*, yes," Sam corrected gently. "Hi."

Sam was on the verge of recognizing the woman when she introduced herself.

"Lynn Cooper," she said, "I'm a reporter for KVDV-TV?"

"I know," Sam said. "Wow, it's great to see you. Jen, she did the story about Tinkerbell and the earthquake!"

"Right!" Jen said, smiling. "I remember."

"'Tinkerbell and the Earthquake.' I just wish I'd thought to call it that," the reporter said, laughing. "It's nice of you to remember."

"Are you kidding?" Sam asked. "It helped Tinkerbell get a home."

"I know you just got here, but did you see him with Katie Sterling?" Lynn asked, gesturing with her coffee cup. "Duke Fairchild's here, too, taking credit for saving Tinkerbell's life."

"It's true," Sam said seriously. "If he hadn't put in the high bid for Tinkerbell at his own auction yard—" Sam broke off.

The gentle giant of a horse had almost been bought for pet food. She shuddered, and was just about to change the subject when an idea glimmered in her mind. She'd made money selling Tinkerbell to Katie Sterling. Maybe the three-thousand-dollar therapy horse didn't have to be Ace. It couldn't be Tinkerbell, of course, since he'd proven to be a talented jumping prospect. Just as an idea began to take form in Sam's mind, Jen's voice cut in.

"I guess we do know some people on this drive," Jen said, "and they're not all dudes." Jen winced and gave an embarrassed smile. "No offense, Ms. Cooper."

"Don't be," Lynn said. "I don't even qualify as a dude. Horses scare me. Give me a nice earthquake, flood, or robbery anytime. At least you know to be on your guard. Horses try to fool you with those gentle eyes."

"Really?" Jen asked. "You're really afraid of horses?"

"I don't dislike them," Lynn assured the girls. "And I realize they photograph beautifully and make good stories. When Tinkerbell pulled the barn off the other horse out at your ranch, for instance . . ." Lynn patted her chest as if even the memory touched her heart. "You can't beat that for drama. But those huge feet, big mouths, and even their nostrils . . ." Lynn held her hands in a shape about the size of a basketball, and both Sam and Jen laughed.

"Speaking of drama . . . ," Sam teased.

"It's why I'm in front of the camera instead of behind it," Lynn said with a mock bow. "Seriously, though, why should a beast that big and strong allow itself to be bossed around by someone your size? I'll stick with my Siamese cats, thank you very much."

"Are you just here for the morning?" Sam asked, since Lynn Cooper clearly wasn't following the herd on horseback.

"No, I've been here from the start, but I'm strictly a motorized passenger," Lynn said, pointing.

Sunrise had brightened the camp, so when Sam glanced in the direction Lynn pointed, she couldn't miss the van. Bright orange despite a layer of dust, the vehicle had WIMP WAGON painted on its side in big black letters.

I'd walk home before I rode in that, Sam thought. Jen straightened so suddenly, the blond braids hanging over her shoulders looked like exclamation points. Sam would bet Jen felt the same.

Lynn Cooper recognized their expressions instantly.

"I have no pride," she pretended to whisper. "Besides, the Wimp Wagon has a CD player, air-conditioning, and a couple of built-in cots."

Lynn was about to go on when a muted trill sounded from her pocket. She held a finger in front of her lips, signing the girls to hush, as she fished out her cell phone.

"No one's supposed to have twenty-first-century gadgets. Hal's number-one rule. He already took Mr. Martinez's PDA."

Amazed, Sam asked, "Mr. Martinez? The banker?"

"The same," Lynn said. "Took it away in such a nice, easygoing, for-your-own-good way, that Mr. Martinez actually thanked him for contributing to a more relaxing week!"

She opened the small silver cell phone.

"Hello?" Lynn said. She listened, then closed the phone with a frown. "Even though we have super high-tech equipment that costs more than I make in a month"—Lynn gestured toward the sky—"it's undependable out here."

"But Hal makes an exception for you?" Sam asked.

"Only because it's my job. And even though Hal welcomes the publicity, he's threatened to confiscate the phone unless I'm discreet," Lynn said.

The phone sounded again, and Lynn moved away, searching for better reception.

Hissing water rose up in a steam cloud. Sam and Jen stepped away as the cook doused the campfire beside them.

They'd talked too long, Sam thought. They were the last ones holding plates and cups. Restless hooves and a sudden cacophony of cattle said it was time to mount up.

"Let's go," Sam said anxiously.

"We're fine," Jen said, taking Sam's plate and slipping it, along with hers, into a bucket of dishwater the cook had indicated. "We're saddled up and our horses know what they're doing."

Sam exhaled. Jen was right. There was no reason for this sudden surge of panic.

"Where?" Lynn Cooper snapped.

Sam wheeled to see the reporter frowning. Her cell phone was clamped between her ear and shoulder as she made notes on a long tablet.

"Any injuries?" she asked. "I said—shoot, this reception's just awful."

Lynn raised one hand to beckon a cameraman mingling with horses and riders.

"I'll catch up with you later," Lynn said, moving toward her tent.

"What happened?" Jen asked after Lynn had hung up.

"Probably nothing serious. I could barely hear, but for some reason they—that was the station calling— want footage and commentary on a one-vehicle accident."

Lynn ducked into her tent, leaving Sam and Jen standing face to face, staring at each other.

"One vehicle?" Sam asked. "How's that possible?"

"I guess someone could have run off the road, not paying attention," Jen said. "Or, since it's early, maybe someone drove all night and fell asleep at the wheel."

Sam nodded. "It's probably no one we know," she said, totally aware she was trying to convince herself as much as Jen was. "After all, Mrs. Allen is the worst driver in northern Nevada and she's still out of town."

Jen gave a tight-lipped smile.

Although Mrs. Allen owned the Blind Faith Mustang Sanctuary and was a friend to wild horses, she was also a living example of how not to drive. Both girls agreed on that.

"Was anyone hurt?" Hal Ryden asked as Lynn emerged with a huge purse slung over her shoulder and a black blazer in one hand.

Where had he come from? Sam wondered, but Lynn didn't look surprised.

"I doubt it," Lynn answered. "But if someone was, I don't want to be dressed for the rodeo. On camera, this will strike a more somber note." Lynn paused.

There was a snap as she shook dust and wrinkles from the blazer.

Sam bit her lower lip as she made sense of Lynn's words.

"You'll wear black, so in case someone—"

"Samantha," Lynn sounded surprised and a little shaken, "all I heard was that there's been a rollover on the highway near War Drum Flats. It's probably no big deal."

Sam sucked in her breath. War Drum Flats was awfully close to home. Lynn's words were making things worse, not better.

"The friend who dropped us off would be about there by now," Jen said.

Would he? How far back would Jake have driven?

Not that she wanted to know.

Sam refused to ask if the rollover involved a pickup truck faded to the color of old denim. She really wished Jen had just ignored the possibility that Jake had been hurt. That's what she was trying to do.

When Lynn glanced at Hal Ryden with a questioning look, Jen grabbed Sam's hand and squeezed.

I don't want to hear this, Sam thought, but Lynn Cooper was already talking.

"The police dispatcher did say the accident involved a horse trailer."

Chapter Three ❧

$\mathcal{S}$am's heart was plummeting when Hal Ryden extended his palm in an abrupt "halt" gesture.

"Girls, experts are on the scene of that accident and I need your help here," he said as Lynn and her cameraman piled into a four-wheel-drive station wagon to leave.

"Okay," Sam managed.

"It'll take a good thirty minutes for this bunch to catch their horses, saddle, and bridle 'em," Hal continued.

Across the camp, the horses were in high spirits. They'd spotted the would-be riders and neighed in mock terror before racing laps around a rope corral.

"After three days they're gettin' the hang of it,"

Hal said, nodding toward the people who stood quietly with halters, waiting for the horses to settle down, before easing in among them.

Ears flicking in all directions, the saddle herd pressed close together, then scattered, but their would-be riders didn't give up.

"Meantime, I'd like you two to scout the mountaintop trail real quick," Hal said. "Make sure nothing up there will spook the cattle before I turn 'em loose."

Sam knew it didn't take much to startle range cattle. A shout, a sudden movement, even an object out of place like an abandoned tire protruding from the sand, could frighten them.

"It's just a precaution," Hal Ryden added. "These rodeo bovines are used to hearing lotsa noise—clapping, whooping, music. You name it. And my horses do fine handling 'em. That's why inexperienced folks are required to ride one of my horses on the drive instead of bringing one of their own."

Good idea, Sam thought.

"We'll ride up there, check things out, and be back before you know it."

Jen's cheery confidence kept Sam from giving Ace a melancholy hug when she stood beside him seconds later.

Few strangers would glance at Ace and see a great horse. Just fourteen hands tall, with a freeze brand on his neck and faint bite scars on his rump, the bay mustang didn't look like anything special.

"You ready?" Jen called, curbing Silly's eagerness to be off by walking her in small circles.

"Just a second," Sam told Jen.

Pretending to adjust his headstall, Sam pushed Ace's coarse black forelock aside and looked at the white marking beneath.

Could you wish on the star on a horse's forehead? Sam sighed.

"If I could, I'd wish you weren't such a great horse," she whispered to him.

Then she kissed Ace's nose. Who cared if anyone was watching?

The trail out of camp grew steep in a hurry, but it was easy to follow as it cut through the changing vegetation. In minutes, Sam and Jen were riding beside a mountain's rock face. As the horses climbed higher, the air turned crisp and sweet as stream water.

The trail was wide enough that the girls could have ridden side by side, but they didn't. Because he was calmer, Ace led while Silly followed a few horse lengths behind.

With only rock on her right, Sam noticed the plants clustered on the hillside to her left. Dust covered the leaves of some plant she didn't recognize.

Stones clattered and brush cracked up ahead.

"Deer?" Sam asked, glancing over her shoulder at Jen.

"Probably," Jen answered. "I don't think we're high enough for mountain sheep, and if it was a cougar, we wouldn't hear it."

"That's comforting," Sam said. Her tone was sarcastic, but her scalp tightened and chills rained down her neck as she checked the rock wall, too.

"Sorry," Jen apologized, wincing.

It had been almost a year since a young cougar had attacked Sam as she rode through Lost Canyon. In nightmares, she still felt the impact against her spine and the yank as the starving cat had pulled her backward, off Strawberry, to the ground.

But when she was awake, she was mostly over it.

"It's okay," Sam said. "A cougar's not going to be crashing through the brush." Then, noticing Silly's wide eyes and flaring nostrils, she added, "I guess it could be mustangs."

"They're just excited," Jen said, sounding preoccupied. "Do you think this is far enough? I mean, there's no landslide or anything. I'm sure they can get the herd and riders through here with no trouble."

As Ace and Silly huffed uphill, Sam stopped watching the far peaks, still tipped with snow, and studied the terrain around them. In the underbrush she glimpsed swatches of purple and crimson, but it wasn't until both horses stopped, nostrils quivering, that Sam recognized the wild roses and thistles.

Pretty and unexpected, they were also sharp with thorns and stickers. She and Jen had better make sure the cattle didn't detour for a spiny snack.

"What is it, girl?" Jen asked her horse.

She leaned forward and pressed her cheek against the mare's golden neck, staring in the same direction.

Through knees resting against her saddle, Sam felt Ace draw a deep breath. His black-tinged ears pricked forward and a shiver ran down his neck. He wasn't winded. He was excited.

Suddenly a nicker rang out ahead of them. The trail curved, so they couldn't see the horse, but Ace and Silly answered before the high-pitched sound faded to an echo.

Probably not a mustang, Sam thought. Wild horses were quieter than domesticated ones.

"Maybe one of Mr. Ryden's other hands rode out earlier," Jen said in a normal tone. She gathered her reins and eased Silly past Ace. "Let's go see."

Insulted that Silly had taken the lead, Ace surged after the palomino. Sam didn't stop him.

Ace slid to a stop just the same, when Silly ducked her head in a half buck.

"Knock it—" Jen's voice broke off in a gasp.

Reining Ace over so she could see past Jen, Sam realized the trail gradually widened as it started downhill again. About a quarter mile away, a beautiful horse stood in the middle of the path. She fidgeted and tossed her head, deciding whether to come uphill and greet the horses that had returned her call.

Alert and cautious, the mare considered the

horses and riders. Her chocolate-brown coat shone with good health. Her flaxen mane hung like an ivory shawl over a neck darkened by sweat. Sam tried to guess at her breed, but couldn't. The mare's wide chest and sloping shoulders should make her smooth-gaited and full of stamina.

As Sam studied the horse's dramatic chocolate-and-cream coloring, she saw signs that the mare had traveled some distance to reach this quiet spot in the mountains.

This was no mustang. From trimmed whiskers to gentle, interested gaze, everything said she'd been cared for, and kindly.

"Hey, girlie," Jen called, extending her arm, fingers loosely closed over her palm.

The dark mare was no stranger to handheld treats, either. She started up the trail.

A domineering snort stopped her.

The mare wasn't alone.

I might have guessed, Sam thought. As the stallion stepped from the lowest curve in the road, the Phantom's beauty turned away her irritation. Even in the watery yellow light of morning, he looked half-magical, a creature made of bone, sinew, and moonbeams.

Sam sighed just as Jen demanded, "What's he doing here?"

"Like you're surprised he found her before we did," Sam said quietly. She hoped Jen would take the hint and keep her voice down. Each sighting of the Phantom was a gift.

With an easy, ambling gait, the mare approached the silver stallion. The horses' ears flicked a message back and forth, then they both broke into a trot. A few strides later, they accelerated into a long, graceful gait just short of a gallop.

"Listen to her," Jen said.

The mare's hooves struck in a graceful four-beat rhythm. Sam heard the unfamiliar cadence even as the horses ran in step, necks aligned, so that their manes—his silver and hers white-gold—billowed back like waves.

All at once, the Phantom's legs reached a little farther and slanted across the mare's path.

"He's trying to cut her off," Jen muttered.

And take her home to his hidden valley, Sam thought.

Instead of letting herself be herded off the open path, though, the mare stopped.

Surprised, the stallion took a few yards to slow to a walk, then arched his neck and, lifting his knees in a proud display, trotted an arc to come back and face her.

Even from this distance, Sam could read the mare's gentle demeanor: She stared at the Phantom with pricked ears. Then she took a step forward and touched his extended muzzle with her own.

Sam smiled. The mare wanted to be friends, but

she didn't want to be pushed around. When he drew near enough, she gave his mane a nibble.

"The Phantom's got a new girlfriend," Jen said in a singsong voice.

To Sam, it was no joke. And Jen knew better than to tease about this. If the mare had been wild, that would be one thing. But she wasn't.

Once before the stallion had been accused of stealing domestic mares, but the accusation had proven false. And just last month, Linc Slocum's mare Hotspot had joined the Phantom's herd after she'd escaped from the thief who'd stolen her and her foal.

Where had this glossy, stable-fed beauty come from?

Head high, the silver stallion acted as if he deserved the affectionate nuzzling.

Jen broke Sam's trance by jostling her arm. The movement stirred Ace, too, and he gave a "What's this?" snort.

"We really should go back," Jen said, then added, "No way, Silly."

Jen's amused tone alerted Sam to the palomino's expression. She stared spellbound at the horses on the trail below as if they were performing just for her.

"I know," Sam said.

The stallion must have heard Sam's voice, because he stepped away from the mare's grooming nibbles and stared up the hillside. Sam didn't move, but her heart rejoiced. Just days ago, the Phantom couldn't have heard a thunderclap. Now he recognized her voice and stood waiting for some sign between them.

Zanzibar. Could the stallion's secret name float like a feather on a gust of wind, leaving her mind to drift to the wild stallion's? As if it could, he tossed his heavy mane back and pawed the mountain path.

But then, it was as if Sam had vanished.

The stallion had no more time for humans. The mare beside him must be added to his herd. Now.

This time the stallion flattened his ears. Then he lowered his head and snaked it close to the mare's mahogany legs, threatening to nip.

For the first time, the mare's ears lay back along her neck and she returned the warning with a clack of her teeth.

Startled, the Phantom looked back over his shoulder, as if she couldn't possibly be snapping at him.

"We really should go, but this is too good," Jen said, covering her lips against a laugh.

Should Sam feel sorry for the stallion?

No, she thought in the next instant. He'd just begun to flirt.

Arching his neck and tucking his chin until it bumped his chest, the Phantom showed off his prance. Then, with ears still laid back, he rocked into a lope. If he could have seen the newly risen sun glinting off the dapples that glittered beneath his hide like silver coins, he would have been even more arrogant.

"It's not going to work," Jen said.

It turned out she was right.

As soon as the Phantom lowered his head again, the mare's ears flattened into her mane and her tail swished in irritation.

Fed up with her stalling, the stallion tried to bully her. His silver shoulder struck her chocolate one. She gave a high-pitched squeal before kicking out a hind hoof.

The stallion shied, then circled her at a slow trot.

"I can hear him thinking from here," Jen joked. "He can't believe it. The almighty Phantom's getting the cold shoulder."

Rejection didn't sit well with the silver stallion.

His trot lengthened, and then he was galloping, tightening his circle around the mare. She shifted and gave a nervous nicker. When he heard her uncertainty, the stallion charged.

Was he planning to ram into the mare, push her off the path, and propel her through the brush, back to his herd? If he collided with the mare's hindquarters, she'd have no choice.

The chocolate mare didn't feel like taking his orders.

When two hind hooves lashed out just beneath the stallion's nose, he slid to a stop.

"That woulda hurt," Jen said as the Phantom veered away.

Still moving at a trot, the mustang shook his head, clearing the ropey mane and forelock from his eyes.

"He'll leave," Sam said. "He can't take a chance on being injured."

For the good of the herd, he had to stay strong.

Suddenly, the Phantom wheeled away and crashed into the brush at the side of the trail. The herbal scent of crushed sagebrush filled the air as he stopped and looked back at the reluctant mare. He gave a buck, and powdery soil swirled around him. As the dust cleared, he tilted his head to one side and his mouth was open.

To Sam, he looked playful as a pup.

Follow me and you won't be sorry, he seemed to say.

But the mare couldn't know about the secret green valley with its cold stream and soaring red rock walls. She stood her ground, watching him.

Giving arrogance one last try, the Phantom rose into a rear. His strong front legs struck at the air.

How could she resist? Sam wondered.

But she did. The chocolate-brown mare was not impressed with the stallion's rearing strength.

"Smart girl," Jen said.

When he came back to earth, the stallion stood

still. He might have been carved from white quartz as he waited.

But the mare looked right through him.

Finally, without a flicker of interest in Sam or Ace, the Phantom trotted away, forcing a path through a crackling thicket of wild roses.

Chapter Four ∾

"**W**hose horse is she?" Sam asked.

As the mare searched for graze, sun danced on her dark brown coat. She stretched her neck to reach, bite, and chew. She clearly hadn't chosen a reunion with humans on horses over the Phantom. The mare seemed content on her own.

"I don't know," Jen said slowly. "I'm still trying to figure out what breed she is. What do you think?"

"I'm no expert compared to you, Jen," Sam said. "I'm not even sure what color she is! Would you call her a chestnut? I mean, she has a dark body with a flaxen mane and tail."

"I guess," Jen said. "But that coloring is distinctive.

It's just—shoot, I've lived in the sticks for so long, I just don't know."

"Wait," Sam said, remembering the sound of the horses running side by side. "Didn't you notice something about her gait?"

"Yeah," Jen said, "but we need to talk with someone who's been around different breeds. Maybe Katie Sterling." Jen sighed. "I'll tell you, Sam, I'm disgusted by my own ignorance. If I'm ever going to be a vet, I have to study horses, not just ride them."

"Don't be so hard on yourself," Sam said, but she didn't say the rest of what she was thinking. *You're a fourteen-year-old girl who's lived in northern Nevada your entire life.*

"Since I'm a student by nature," Jen said, blinking slowly behind the shiny disks of her glasses, "and we don't have the HARP girls this week, I'll go to the library, load up on books, and cram some horse information into my brain. Not like that will be unpleasant."

Silly lowered her head and blew out a long breath.

"Yes, girl," Jen joked with her palomino. "We're both relieved to have a plan. Now, let's get back to the campground before Hal thinks we've defected."

"But what about her?" Sam asked. "She's obviously someone's horse. We can't just leave her there."

The mare looked quite satisfied, but that didn't mean someone wasn't looking for her. Any horse would enjoy similar surroundings.

Even Ace.

Sam rubbed her horse's neck while she tried to erase a totally immature thought. The idea refused to vanish. What if Ace "escaped" and returned to the Phantom's herd? He couldn't be sold as a therapy horse then, could he?

No. No way would she duck her responsibility. That would be so selfish, so juvenile, so . . .

"Ridiculous."

"What is?" Jen asked.

Sam bit her lip. She hadn't meant to say the word out loud.

"Nothing," Sam said. "I was just thinking it would be pointless to try to rope her and bring her in now. She'll probably see all the other horses as we drive the herd through here, and join up."

For a second, Jen hesitated.

She's not reading my mind, Sam told herself. Jen had been asleep this morning when she'd told Jake about the offer to buy Ace.

"Good point," Jen said, proving she was just weighing the logic of Sam's statement. "Even if she doesn't fall in with the herd, we can report her to Sheriff Ballard."

And it was settled. But thinking about this morning had stirred another worry. What about the accident Lynn Cooper had rushed off to cover?

Jake was a very careful driver, but if an animal

had run into the road in front of him, he'd surely swerve to miss it.

"Jen, you don't think that accident with the horse trailer . . . ?" Sam couldn't force herself to finish the sentence.

"No way," Jen said. "He's towing your dad's trailer. He'd never risk Wyatt's good opinion of him. Besides, if Jake were in trouble, he wouldn't call the sheriff."

Sam couldn't help giggling as she pictured Jake walking for help, muttering that buckaroos should never do anything except on horseback.

"Sam, it wasn't him. Don't even think about it," Jen said.

At a touch, Jen had Silly swinging into an about-face, headed back toward camp. Sam turned Ace and followed.

As they rode down, the herd of cattle was coming up the trail.

The horned heads of the leaders marked them as steers used in the rodeo's bulldogging event, but most of the others were Hereford cows and calves, which would be used in the roping competitions.

Two outriders wearing black shirts with blue-green script spelling out "Ryden Rodeo Productions" flanked the herd.

They don't look like they need a bit of help, Sam thought.

"Hal's riding drag, waiting for your report," one of the riders called out as they approached.

Jen touched her hat brim like the experienced hand she was, but Sam just smiled as they rode past.

Jen gestured for Sam to ride down one side of the herd while she rode down the other. They split up, Sam figured, because a single rider disturbed the herd less than two of them would. Cattle, like most prey animals, responded to possible danger by moving away from it. Wild cattle perceived even faint hand movements from a rider on a ridge as a hazard. Sam had learned that the hard way.

But this herd stayed calm.

Nodding and plodding, the cattle moved at a steady pace, ignoring the chatter of less experienced riders ranged along the side of the herd.

Ace danced with impatience. He obeyed her hands and legs, heading steadily for the rear of the herd, but if a horse could trot on the tips of his hooves, he was.

"They're getting along fine without you," she told the bay, but the words were no sooner out of her mouth than she heard what she'd said.

Sam leaned down until her chin touched Ace's coarse black mane, and whispered, "They are, but I could never get along without you."

Just the thought of losing Ace made her heart feel empty, but the gelding was in no mood to think of anything but cows.

As they jogged past two riders, Sam overheard them talking.

"What are those little white-faced ones with the perpetual 'Huh?' expression on their faces?" the dude asked.

"Them's Herefords, ma'am. And the rest of the herd is kinda mixed. We've got Charolais, Brahma, and Angus, but mostly crosses of some kind."

Suddenly Ace's head tilted right, as if he were listening. But he wasn't eavesdropping. He'd noticed a horse ridden many lengths out from the herd. Ace sucked in a long draught of air, analyzing it for the horse's scent.

The other horse was a huge bay. He moved at a walk, but his ears pricked forward with eagerness. He'd come a long way from the neglected animal with a tangled mane and bleeding poll who'd almost been sold for pet food, but Sam recognized him.

"Tinkerbell!" Sam gasped, then turned Ace toward the giant horse.

On the first day she'd seen Tinkerbell, he'd acted clumsy and ashamed of his size. The men handling him had called him a "big oaf" as they unloaded him from a too-small trailer. None of the tack at River Bend had fit him, and even when Sam had led him into the biggest box stall in the barn, he'd filled it up.

But those days were over. Grooming, good food, and gentle care had helped, but when Tinkerbell had shown Sam that jumping was what he was meant to do, everything had changed. Now the gelding moved at a rocking canter. He looked proud as a circus horse circling the center ring in the big top.

"Katie!" Sam called out to his rider.

Katie Sterling always dressed in the practical clothes of a working horsewoman, yet she managed to look like a fashion model. Sterling Stables was known for its select Morgan performance horses, but Katie's knowledge of all things equine was practically famous. Sam wished she could tell Katie about the mare on the mountain.

But there was no time. As Sam looked over the heads of the massed cattle, she saw that Jen's tan cowgirl hat had almost reached the rear of the herd.

Sam gave a quick wave at Katie and rode on.

At the back of the herd, Hal rode with a group of men. Sam recognized most of them, including Linc Slocum, Duke Fairchild, and Mr. Martinez.

Duke Fairchild's mount was an iron-gray Quarter Horse, and Mr. Martinez rode Teddy Bear, the part–Bashkir Curly gelding who'd been schooled for him by Jake and Dad. But Linc wasn't astride his palomino, Champ.

For a minute Sam wondered where the sedate dun Linc rode had come from. Then she noticed the black-and-teal halter the horse wore under his bridle and remembered that Hal Ryden required all inexperienced riders to ride his horses.

Ouch, Sam thought. Linc Slocum wanted everyone

to think of him as a true Westerner, but a member of Ryden Rodeo Productions had determined that Linc wasn't a skilled enough horseman to ride his own horse.

If Linc was embarrassed, though, you'd never guess it from the way he was acting. He leaned back in the saddle as if it were a recliner in front of a television. His grip on the reins was the only thing keeping him from falling back over his horse's rump.

"Why, I guess I am somethin' of a newcomer," Linc was saying to Duke Fairchild. "But I swear I've been out here, horseback riding across this great land of ours so often, I know all the lizards by their first names!"

Caught up in his performance, Linc probably didn't notice the dun's gaping mouth as he fought the bit's pull.

Someone had to say something. Sam remembered playing in the tack room as a child, putting a bit in her mouth and holding it there so that she could feel the cold weight of it. How old had she been? She couldn't remember that—just that it hadn't been so bad until she'd asked Jake to tug on the reins so she could see how it felt. Maybe he'd been a little too enthusiastic at the task, because even now, she recalled the gagging sensation and the ache, as if her jaw joint was parting from her skull.

Enough, Sam thought, but Hal Ryden acted more quickly than she did.

Urging his black gelding forward, Hal reined in beside Linc and winked at him.

"Ease up a little bit there, partner," he said. "That pony's used to loose cow horse reins."

Thank goodness, Sam thought. And she hadn't said a word—so why was Linc giving her a glare?

Just because she was a witness to his embarrassment? That didn't make any sense, especially when he was riding with people he'd consider a lot more important. Duke Fairchild's auction yard had made him affluent, according to Dad, and Mr. Martinez was a bank officer in Darton. He collected exotic horses, just like Linc did. Of course, he actually rode them, while Linc just boasted he possessed rare animals, like his imported Shetland ponies.

Maybe Linc thought he'd cemented their good opinion of him when he'd earned a place on the rodeo association board. Sam would bet he was wrong.

"Everything okay, girls?" Hal called, spotting Sam and Jen before they reached him.

They were nodding, ready to tell him all about the mare, when he gestured them back toward the herd.

"Go where you're needed, then," he said. "And keep your eyes open."

Sam and Jen looked at each other and gave faint shrugs. Before each could return to her side of the herd, Linc echoed, "Yeah, you'd best keep your eyes open, little ladies. Everythin' out here bites, scratches, or spits. And I'm not just talkin' about the cowboys!"

Ace bolted and Sam let him go. She heard the sandy soil churn under his hooves and knew her quick departure was bad manners, but if Ace was too smart to stick around when Linc started running his mouth, shouldn't she be, too?

As Ace fell in beside the herd, Sam smiled. She'd missed the spring cattle drive this year because she'd had to stay home with Dark Sunshine, who had been about to give birth. It had been a good choice, because she'd been the only one there when Tempest was born, but now she realized how much she loved the steady, even pace of the cattle and their individual personalities.

There, walking against the tide of the other animals, a tender mother cow lowed in her own special voice, calling to her calf. Sam and Ace passed another mother, summoning her baby with a trumpeting sound that might have been an elephant's. A third sounded just like the air horn her friend Pam's mom had taken to basketball games at her old middle school. The babies sounded more alike, making a chorus of *maaa* sounds.

Responding to some sign Sam didn't recognize, half the herd stopped.

White-faced calves nursed.

Up ahead, the rest of the herd moved more

slowly. Now was the time she should ride back up to the front, Sam thought, but she had to stay and watch this peaceful moment. When things were this still, you could hear the buzzing of a few flies and the whisking of tiny tails.

Sam expected the calves to nap after they'd filled their tummies. Instead, they broke into a frisky, heel-swiveling stampede.

"Psycho time," said one of the dudes, but the burst of energy faded quickly.

Five minutes later, all the babies were walking drowsily beside their mothers.

During this lull, Sam suddenly remembered something that eased her worry over Jake.

This morning as they'd been driving toward Pinion Pine camp, Jake had thought he'd heard a siren.

Sirens on the range were rare. That's why Jake hadn't even been certain he'd heard one. The sound of a coyote or calling bird would have been more likely. But Jake's senses were acute, trained to help him as a tracker.

She'd bet he'd been right about the siren. And if he was, it must have been Sheriff Ballard's car going to the accident even before Jake had dropped them off.

The trail started downhill. There was no sign of the chocolate-brown mare, but far in the distance, a field of lupine looked like a purple cloud.

Jake was safe. She just knew it.

"Oh yeah," Sam said, spinning the ends of her reins in delight.

Spotting the blur of reins from the corner of his eye, Ace shied.

"I'm sure you're terrified," she teased the horse.

Feeling her elation, the little mustang lowered his head and gave a crow-hopping buck.

"Ride 'em, cowgirl!" called one of the dudes.

Sam's spirits soared, but she stayed in the saddle.

She was ready for Ace's sassiness. Or anything else that might come.

Chapter Five ❧

Ace was the first member of the Darton Rodeo cattle drive to set hoof on asphalt as they rode out of the mountains, onto the flat range, and finally into a rural neighborhood.

Though it was Friday afternoon, lots of people lined the street. Twin boys, holding leashes for identical barking puppies, stood beside a girl in a striped T-shirt with a skateboard tucked under her arm. Three mothers stood together. One held a baby perched on her hip, while another scooted a stroller back and forth as the baby inside bounced in excitement. The third mother held the hands of lunging toddlers mooing greetings to the cows.

"Good thinking," Sam commented to Ace when

she saw that one enterprising girl had set up a lemonade stand.

Ace wasn't amused by all the excitement. He mouthed his bit nervously, even when Sam rubbed his withers.

He gave a worried snort as a boy flipped a Frisbee over the herd to his friend on the opposite sidewalk.

"Hey now," Sam chided Ace. "You've put up with snowstorms, wild animals, and gunshots. This is nothing."

"It's like a parade," Jen called from her own position up front.

Since she could feel Ace growing more nervous with every step, Sam didn't shout back. She just nodded.

The closer they got to Darton, the more people crowded the sidewalks. As they left the first neighborhood, a police car cruised quietly ahead, leading them down a street that linked with Fairground Way.

The other streets were blocked off to traffic. Sawhorses and flapping signs directed drivers to detours.

The steer-wrestling cattle led the way, tossing their heads as if they were trying to look like Old West longhorns. As Hal Ryden had requested, Sam and Jen rode point, up front on each side.

It was about two o'clock and Sam was starving. It seemed like forever since breakfast. Now the aroma of popcorn and corn dogs wafted from the fairgrounds and she smiled, remembering the money

Dad had given her to cover "expenses" before he arrived to pick her up after the rodeo. Hal Ryden had said they could go as his guests.

The blare of a car horn sent Ace side stepping toward the herd.

"Idiot," Sam muttered at the driver who must have ignored all of the detour signs. She hoped the police issued him a ticket.

Shaking her head, Jen called across the herd, "Doesn't it seem like he mighta noticed the flags and horses and one hundred head of cattle?"

A cream-colored calf bolted from the herd.

Before Sam could react, Ace sprinted after it, hooves hammering the asphalt. Though the retrieval only took a few seconds, Ace felt better for it. He came trotting back to the herd, acting more like himself.

"That's what you do best, isn't it, boy?" Sam crooned to her horse.

Ahead, she noticed a lean woman with cameras slung bandolier-style over her shoulders. She sighted through a camera, shooting away as the press pass around her neck swayed. She must be a newspaper photographer, Sam thought, and couldn't resist the envy that fizzed up in her.

Sam pictured the cattle as they'd look through the camera's viewfinder. Wild-eyed and doe-eyed. Tiny dancing hooves and big black cloven hooves. The contrasts were what she'd shoot. That would be a good idea for photographing the people, too. If she were doing this story for the school newspaper, her photo essay would investigate who'd signed up to relive this bit of the historical West and why.

Could you major in photojournalism in college? It was a long way in the future, but Sam thought it could be exciting.

Where was Lynn Cooper? She'd said she was covering the cattle drive, but then she'd been called away.

Sam shivered at the memory of the black blazer Lynn had brought along "just in case" and wondered what she'd found when she'd arrived at the desolate piece of road where a truck had rolled over with a horse trailer.

Still holding her reins, Sam crossed her fingers, hoping the trailer had been empty and the driver hadn't been hurt.

An air horn blatted from the sidewalk crowd, and Ace's flat-footed stride faltered.

"You're doing fine, boy," Sam said. "Humans can just be stupid. You'd think they'd be smart enough to find some other way to show they're excited, wouldn't you?"

The fairgrounds were in sight when Sam heard Lynn Cooper's voice and glanced over her shoulder to see the blond reporter with the KVDV cameraman.

Keeping her distance from the horses, Lynn walked along quickly, calling out questions to the dudes.

"So what would you bring next time that you forgot?" Lynn asked two middle-aged women who were riding together.

"Mosquito repellent," answered one.

"Actually, I could have gotten away with less," answered the other. "Chaps keep your jeans pretty clean."

"What did you like best about the trip?" Lynn asked a man Sam had spotted earlier. Even in cowboy gear, he looked like an accountant.

"One thing that I really enjoyed was being able to zone out. I had a job to do, but no responsibilities beyond my horse and me." He leaned down and patted the neck of a sturdy bay.

A woman with the skinniest eyebrows Sam had ever seen reined her sorrel gelding over to talk with Lynn. The woman rode better than most of the dudes, and Sam could see a silk scarf tied over her hair, under her hat.

"I read about this in the business news section of the paper, and in the city I only ride maybe once each month. So I signed up to have some quality time with my horse.

"The first day, I couldn't help looking at my watch every five minutes, but after I took it off and put it in my saddlebag, I found out Cheyenne here really likes my rendition of 'I'm an Old Cow Hand.'"

Lynn thanked her and glanced at the cameraman.

"Got it?" Lynn asked. When he nodded, she

suggested, "Why not go up where the cows turn into the parking lot? Catch the girls in front. They're local and they look great."

Sam knew she was smiling when Lynn jogged toward her, not at all out of breath, and gave her a thumbs-up.

"Hi," Sam said. She wanted to say something clever and sociable, but all she could think about was the rollover.

"It wasn't old and blue, was it?" she asked hopefully, and Lynn knew exactly what she was talking about.

"Nope," Lynn said. "Old and yellow with Arizona license plates. It's a"—she flipped back a page of her notebook—"restored 1968 Scout. And hard as it is to believe, there was hardly a scratch on it. According to the sheriff, the driver—a college student—said she was fine. She hitched a ride to town, where she planned to call her boyfriend to come get her."

Sam's shoulders sagged and her chest deflated with her sigh.

"That is so good," she said. The words were mild compared to the relief she felt.

She'd been listening so intently to Lynn, though, she hadn't heard Ace's hooves skittering on the asphalt. Now she did, and lifted her reins a little, making contact with his mouth.

"I'm still here, boy," she said, then she glanced

across the herd. She had to tell Jen it hadn't been Jake's truck.

Jen had drawn rein to let a few girls pet Silly's shoulder. While the palomino basked in the attention, Sam caught Jen's eye. At once, Jen took in Lynn, then Jen tilted her head to one side. Sam gave her an okay sign.

Jen's smile flashed across the herd. She lifted her Stetson above her hair and whirled it around one finger as if she'd throw it skyward.

That's the sign of a good friend, Sam thought. She's celebrating for me, even though she never really shared my fears.

"Her horse seems pretty laid-back about all this," Lynn said.

Sam heard the comparison in Lynn's words, even though it wasn't exactly criticism.

"All the Kenworthy palominos have been in parades before," Sam said. "Sometimes they ride together as a family."

"And your horse never has," Lynn said.

"He's a mustang," Sam explained. "First he lived on the range and now he lives at River Bend, our ranch. As far as I know, this is the most civilization he's ever seen."

Lynn cast a glance around them and gave a "not bad" nod, then fell back a few yards when Ace side stepped toward her.

"You're doing fine," Sam said, but then, as if to

test her words, a little boy, maybe a fourth grader, scampered into Ace's path.

Apparently the boy had pulled away from his mother. From the corner of her eye, Sam saw a woman elbowing out of the crowd, running after her child as he approached Ace, hand outstretched.

His hand wasn't empty. In fact, it didn't take Sam or Ace long to realize the child was holding a snake.

"Don't—" Sam tried not to shout. Ace needed her to stay calm.

"It's just a garter snake. It won't bite," the boy insisted. "That flickery thing is just his tongue. His mouth isn't even open. It's his ola-olafactory—"

The boy's mother grabbed him around the middle and lifted him off his feet. Blushing and apologizing, she carried him, snake and all, back to the sidewalk.

Sam started to lean forward to rub Ace's neck, then changed her mind. Instead, she gave him the sort of atta-boy pat Jake or Dad would use. Ace wouldn't expect it, and the surprise might keep his attention focused on her.

"You're a good horse," Sam told him.

Snorting and rumbling, Ace veered closer to the cattle. He knew what *they* were all about.

Sam couldn't wait to reach the fairgrounds. Ace had had enough.

A disturbance came from the back of the herd, but Sam didn't even look. Ace felt tense beneath her.

They were riding on asphalt. He could bolt and slip. Anything could happen. There was no way she'd risk a disaster because Linc Slocum was causing trouble as usual.

That probably wasn't fair, Sam thought. In fact, when she considered the calm dun he'd been riding, she guessed she was wrong.

One quick glance over the stream of curly-headed calves behind her showed Sam that Hal Ryden was standing in his stirrups.

"He's got it under control," Sam told Ace, but her horse's ears didn't even flick back to catch her voice.

Ace was definitely out of his comfort zone. Sam only hoped she'd progressed enough as a rider to keep him together.

As they took a turn toward the parking lot, Sam smelled deep-fried carnival food amid the scents of hay and livestock. Perhaps Ace was comforted by the smell of other horses or maybe he just realized lots of eyes were watching him with admiration, because he blew through his lips and pranced.

Men with walkie-talkies waved them by a sign that said MUST SHOW PASS.

"Almost there, boy," Sam told her horse.

Hal had said to herd the cattle into the arena. From there, the animals would be sorted into the appropriate corrals by his staff. Most of the corrals and one entire barn were reserved for rodeo stock, and Hal had offered to let Jen and Sam strip the tack from their horses, cool them out, and keep them in his stalls until Dad arrived to trailer them home.

Sam tried to slam a mental door on thoughts of home. Amelia's grandmother had been in a hurry for her answer about Ace. What if she'd called back and talked with Gram? What if the decision had already been made for her?

Ace broke out of his flat-footed walk and into a trot. He looked back over his left shoulder.

You're okay, boy, Sam thought. This time she told him with hands and legs, hoping that the silence a mustang depended on for safety was the right way.

Ace looked back again with pricked ears and flared nostrils.

Nothing back there that you haven't seen before, she told him with her thoughts, hoping it was true.

Finally Sam snugged her reins. Ace ignored her, so she tightened them until they ran in straight lines to his bit. The gelding shook his head from side to side, yanking in short jerks, quickening his pace before swerving left again.

Was he trying to unseat her, or was there really something back there?

With all the cars, pedestrians, and flapping posters stapled to bulletin boards, Sam knew she should be looking up ahead, but then Ace lifted his knees in a trot.

Ignoring her, he only went faster, past rows of cars and horse trailers, gathering speed though he was mincing sideways.

Finally, Sam followed his stare and saw what Ace was watching.

The mountain mare had followed them. Sun shone on her chocolate coat, making pinkish flickers. She looked determined, as if she knew exactly where she was going and what she'd do when she got there. And yet the mare's pace was unhurried and so smooth, her tawny mane barely ruffled and her tail drifted only at the tip.

She's coming along. Okay. No need to think about her, Sam thought.

Then, for the hundredth time, Sam ordered herself to worry about what was in front of her.

But she was too late.

A creak sounded on their right and a car door burst open just a few feet away.

Hands steady on Ace's reins, Sam saw a flash of a sundress, watermelon pink and green. Then a little girl rushed into Ace's path.

With her hand extended toward Ace's nose, the girl shouted, "Can I pet him?"

As Ace slid to a cow-horse stop, his shoes grated on asphalt.

He'd stopped in time to miss the child, and though Ace huffed with exertion, it seemed everything was okay until the child's openmouthed father dashed after her.

Ace rose in a half-rear and Sam heard a camera's motor drive whirring through an endless series of photos, capturing Ace rearing over the little girl's head.

Chapter Six ⬥

"It was no big deal," Jen told Sam later as they unsaddled their horses outside the rodeo barn that would provide a home for Ryden Rodeo Productions horses for the next few days.

The fairground had three double barns. Sam and Jen peeked inside theirs and saw that an interior corridor ran between rows of twelve stalls on each side, with a feed room at one end and a tack room at the other. The barn was airy and light, and the horses could look inside the barn or out to the activity of people and animals preparing for tonight's rodeo performance.

As Sam and Jen unsaddled Ace and Silly, a trio of glossy black horses—part of Hal Ryden's arena remuda—stretched their necks over half doors to watch. Their muzzles dripped water, as if instinct had urged them to take greedy swallows from their buckets before the new arrivals could drink. The horses' nostrils were dusted with cedar shavings and the scent of fresh bedding was all around.

"It was, too, a big deal," Sam insisted as she released Ace's cinch, tossed it over the saddle seat, then grabbed the horn and cantle to slide the saddle from her horse's sweating back.

"Nonsense," Jen said. "Just hustle, okay? I want to get back over to the arena. Hal said they'd let the mare stay there, with the other stock until we get there, but—"

"I know." Sam tried not to sound snappish as the saddle blanket, covered in Ace's red-gold hairs, came off with the saddle and fell across her boot toes. Sam kicked it aside. Carefully.

It would be just her luck to trip and fall flat on her face, now, when she had an audience.

On their way to the "Last Roundup" barbecue, sponsored by the Darton Rodeo Association, many of the dudes had already come by to tell Sam how much they admired her dramatic riding. Some thought it had been a Hollywood-style trick. Others thought Ace had acted up and she'd ridden him to a standstill. No one but Jen seemed to see it for what it was: a mistake. All hers.

If she'd been a better rider, she would have seen

at a glance that the chocolate mare was following, then she would have shifted her attention forward where it belonged. She wouldn't have been clawing to stay in the saddle. She wouldn't have nearly fallen. Most of all, she wouldn't have brought a range-bred mustang into town.

Guilt stabbed through her as she touched Ace's wet coat. The little horse was stressed, and she couldn't even give him the comfort of a good brushing. She didn't have a curry comb or dandy brush, and it seemed rude to ask a stranger if she could borrow grooming gear.

Sam unknotted the flannel she'd tied around her waist when it grew too hot, and used it to rub Ace down.

The gelding stared back over his shoulder. His brown eyes looked almost apologetic. His ribs heaved as if he'd run hard.

"It's not your fault, boy. It's mine," she told him.

"Sam, no matter how many times you apologize to him, Ace won't understand," Jen said.

"You don't know that."

"Sure I do. Just watch. In a few minutes, he'll be drinking water, standing in one of these huge box stalls filled with cedar shavings, and he'll have forgotten all about it."

Jen was probably right. Ace rarely held a grudge. But today her mistake had been lots worse than usual.

"How can you be sure?" Sam asked, watching

Jen lead her horse down the barn row to cool off. Silly looked curious and alert, not exhausted like Ace.

"Because it wasn't a traumatic event." Jen's voice floated back to Sam. Then she returned. "He was distracted by the mare, just like you were. When he turned back and saw that girl in his path, he spooked. That's all. Next time he's in a parade or someplace congested like this, he'll know what to expect."

There won't be a next time, Sam thought. *This is one cow pony who'll be staying home.*

Her hands were cold and shaky, despite the temperature. She pressed her palms against Ace's warm hide, feeling comforted even if he didn't.

She led Ace after Silly, and the gelding took easy strides. He'd begun relaxing.

"Samantha Forster, please report to the first aid station."

Both girls stopped. Silly kept walking and only halted when she realized Jen wasn't coming with her.

Sam stared at Jen. Then, slowly, half afraid she'd imagined the official-sounding voice, Sam asked, "Did they just say what it sounded like? My name?"

Jen stared at the public address system as if she'd glimpse a face behind the speaker. Then she nodded.

"Samantha Forster, if you're on the grounds, please report to the first aid station."

"Why would they want me?" Sam asked.

Jen mulled that over as she opened a stall and turned Silly in.

"Obviously you're okay," Jen said then.

"Obviously," Sam answered. "But maybe someone thought I was hurt in that horrible display of non-horsemanship in the parking lot," Sam said.

"Shut up," Jen requested in a sensible tone.

"Or —" Sam felt her stomach dip with fear. "What if that little girl was hurt after all?"

"Will you quit being so paranoid?" Jen scolded. "If she was hurt at all, it was from her dad scooping her up and clamping her in that bear hug against his chest."

"But maybe after he took a closer look at her," Sam began.

"Sam! Snap out of it!" Jen sounded as if she was out of patience.

Sam turned Ace into the stall next to Silly's as Jen kept talking.

"In case you didn't hear him, that father thanked you for 'keeping your horse under control,' remember?"

"Then what is it?"

"Wouldn't it be faster to quit guessing and go see?"

Sam threw down her flannel. Of course, Jen was right.

Sam pretended she didn't see Jen retrieve the flannel shirt and begin folding it. "I don't even know where I'm going," she muttered.

Ace neighed longingly after her.

Horses sure do forgive more easily than people, she thought.

She headed toward a trailer that looked like it had been set up as an office. Could that be the first aid station?

Everyone she passed wore some kind of pass around their neck, or a fluorescent wristband. Clearly she should have one, too. She was hurrying between barns, threading her way past pens packed with Brahma bucking bulls, and there were plenty of men standing around with walkie-talkies, scrutinizing each passerby.

Why didn't anyone stop her?

Had they already circulated her description? Had she been deemed mounted and dangerous?

No, wait. Maybe no one questioned her because she still wore Hal Ryden's black and blue-green trappings. Did they think she belonged here? After all, she had helped bring in a hundred head of rodeo cattle and twenty-two riders.

If she considered it that way, Sam thought, *maybe she did belong here.*

As she drew closer, Sam saw the trailer that she was headed for had a sign on the door. It said MEDIA. Not first aid.

Sam swerved away, then stopped, hands on hips, to stare around. She could see the empty grandstand. Beyond that, the Ferris wheel turned in the carnival area.

"Last call," the metallic voice said again, without a trace of impatience. "Samantha Forster, please report to the first aid station as soon as possible."

Whoever wanted her wasn't giving up. But who could she ask for directions?

Screams of delight wafted to Sam from the mini roller coaster as she realized that the best place to seek help was right behind her.

Reporters would be covering the rodeo all week, and competitors got hurt far too often. Someone in the media trailer would know how to find the first aid station.

Hand raised, Sam stared at the closed door. She was wasting time. Something might really be wrong. Feeling nervous and out of place, Sam knocked on the door. Nothing happened.

If you belonged here, you probably knew to walk right in. Or you used your key.

Sam took a deep breath and held it. What was the worse thing that could happen if she just opened the door and asked her question?

Her fingers had just grazed the knob when the door opened toward her and Lynn Cooper, looking startled, gazed down at her.

"Hey, Sam, I was just going to walk over to the first aid station and see what the excitement was about."

"Excitement?" Sam asked.

"They're paging you," Lynn told her.

"Oh, I know," Sam said, more relieved than embarrassed. "It's just that I don't know where the first aid station is. I was hoping someone in there could point me toward it."

"Come with me," Lynn said. She rested her hand on Sam's shoulder, called to someone inside the trailer that she'd be back, then took long, ground-eating strides across the fairgrounds.

The first thing Sam noticed inside the first aid station was a shirtless cowboy wincing. His ribs were being examined by a white-coated woman's prodding fingers.

"The rodeo doesn't even start until six o'clock," Lynn said. "Are you sure this counts as fun?"

Lynn had been asking Sam, but the young cowboy looked up and drawled, "Yes, ma'am."

Then Sam saw Brynna, her stepmother.

Before the number of things that could be wrong stampeded through Sam's mind, Brynna held up her hand and rippled her fingers in greeting.

"There you are," Brynna said.

Did she sound worried? Angry? Hurt?

None of those. Her tone was businesslike, but that went along with her attire. Brynna was dressed for her job as manager of the Bureau of Land Management's wild horse corrals at Willow Springs—a twenty-minute drive away from here.

With her red hair back in a tight French braid and her uniform shirt bloused over the top of her trousers to accommodate her pregnancy, Brynna gave Sam a smile that said nothing was seriously wrong.

"Come on in," Brynna said, gesturing Sam closer.

Brynna sat next to an examining table, where a dark-haired woman's eyelids were held apart by a doctor wielding a penlight to check her eyes.

Maybe not a woman, Sam thought. She seemed too shy for an adult, looking down as if the examination were totally embarrassing.

She was somewhere between high school and the work world. College, maybe?

"Hi, Lynn," Brynna said, as if she'd just noticed the reporter.

"I'd still be wandering around the barns if Lynn hadn't helped me find you," Sam explained. "We just rode in —"

"I didn't," Lynn protested, "But Samantha is quite the equestrian."

Sam shook her head, then finished, "—and I'd just unsaddled Ace when I heard my name on the loudspeaker. I had no idea where to go or what was wrong."

"I hope I didn't scare you," Brynna said.

"Not too much," Sam said, but she noticed Brynna didn't rush to say nothing was wrong.

In fact, her stepmother glanced away from Sam and back toward the doctor who was examining the dark-haired girl's eyes. He said something like "equal and reactive."

"I just thought as long as I was here, I'd check and see how the drive went," Brynna said, turning back to Sam.

"Great," Sam told her. "Except Ace doesn't like the city much."

"My cameraman caught his great bucking bronco imitation," Lynn joked. "You might catch it on the evening news."

Oh please, no, Sam thought. If Dad saw her on the news and spotted her riding mistakes—Sam shuddered. She didn't want to imagine what he would say. Or do.

Brynna's eyes swept Sam from head to toe, but Sam saw no sign of panic. One thing she appreciated about Brynna—especially compared to Dad and Jake—was her stepmother's willingness to believe Sam could mostly take care of herself.

Or maybe Brynna was preoccupied with the girl on the examining table. Again, Brynna turned back toward the doctor.

"I'm glad I happened to be in," the doctor said, more to Brynna than to the girl. "Usually I don't arrive until just before the events begin."

"Dr. Yung volunteers his time during the rodeo," Brynna put in. "He's an orthopedic surgeon," Brynna explained, as if it were kind of a joke.

Sam wasn't sure, but she thought orthopedic doctors specialized in broken bones.

"I'm really fine, Mrs. Forster," the dark-haired

girl said. She didn't look at Brynna or the doctor. Her eyes fixed on the space between Sam and Lynn.

"This won't take much longer," Brynna assured her.

"Thanks for giving me a lift, but you don't have to stay." The girl sighed, looking as if Brynna had pulled a trick by bringing her to the rodeo doctor. "I'll call Kevin and he'll be here in a couple hours to pick me up."

Although Lynn did nothing but pass her thumb over the notebook she carried, Sam knew the reporter had realized, just as Sam had, that this was probably the girl from the rollover.

Sam looked at her more closely.

Her dark hair was cut short, with curls going every which way. She was cute, but pale and shaken. As the doctor lifted hair away from her temple, Sam wondered if the girl had suffered a head injury.

"Really, I'm fine," she said. She tried to duck away, but the doctor held her steady. "My head's okay." Then, surrendering, she added, "It's my shoulder that hurts."

The girl was fighting tears. Sam could see them shining in her eyes.

It didn't surprise Sam that Brynna saw them, too, and created a diversion.

"Sam, this is Diana McKenzie. She's a student in the school of nursing at the university, and she rides." Brynna smiled at Sam, urging her to join in the distraction.

"Diana, this is my daughter Samantha. She's a horsewoman, too."

Daughter. Ever since Brynna had revealed her pregnancy, she'd referred to Sam as her daughter instead of her stepdaughter. Sam tried to squash down her inappropriate joy, wondering if it was over this acceptance, or the fact that Brynna had called her a horsewoman.

Even though she wasn't, it was cool that Brynna had said it.

"Diana had an accident this morning," Brynna began.

"And your mom was nice enough to give me a ride here." Diana shrunk from the probing over her ear. "They didn't think I should drive, but I really don't want to leave my car—ouch!"

"You took a pretty good knock to the head," the doctor was saying, checking her eyes once more. "Driving might have been a mistake."

"And your car's fine," Lynn said. "If it's the yellow Scout, that is." Diana nodded and Lynn hurried on, "The sheriff had it towed to his office in Darton, but he said there was hardly a scratch on it."

"Oh, thanks," Diana said questioningly.

"I'm Lynn Cooper. I was called out to the scene of the accident to do a news story, but don't worry—" She held up a hand when Diana shrunk away from her. "I'm not working now. I was just being Samantha's guide."

"Uh, but you're doing a story about the accident?" Diana wet her lips. Her face was suddenly red and perspiration dotted her upper lip.

Diana wasn't as untouched by the crash as she thought. Sam recognized shock when she saw it.

"It's her dad's truck and trailer," Brynna explained.

"Ah," Lynn said, nodding. "Well, I'm pretty sure cows stampeding through the streets of town will be a bigger story than your accident."

When Diana didn't smile, Lynn added, "I'm also sure your father would be more concerned about you, wouldn't he?"

"I guess," the girl said on a sigh.

"You're getting the care you need—"

"I'm fine," the girl protested. "I just need to call Kevin."

"—the truck's fine," Lynn went on, "and there was no horse in the trailer, right?"

"No!" Diana's eyes widened and their hazel shade turned almost green. "Of course not." Diana swayed, then purposely straightened her shoulders.

"There wasn't a horse," Diana repeated, as if they hadn't heard her. "I was going to pick up my horse."

Dr. Yung made a "settle down" sound in his throat and glanced toward Brynna. Sam knew that look. It meant the two adults had decided Diana wasn't going anywhere soon.

"Does your Dad live nearby?" Lynn asked.

"He has a horse farm near Phoenix," Diana said, wearily. "Arizona."

Looking worn out, she leaned her palms on her knees and stared at the floor.

"No problem," Lynn said. "This is a small local station. He won't hear about it from me."

Sam watched Diana—and not just because she was afraid she'd pass out and fall forward.

Sam told herself she was suspicious for no reason. She'd had a troubling day, that's all. But if Diana's family farm was in Phoenix and she'd been going to pick up her horse, why had she been driving north, away from Phoenix, with an empty horse trailer?

Sam knew she might have her geography wrong. She wished Jen were here listening, too.

Brynna glanced at her watch. *She should be at work,* Sam thought, *but she didn't seem to be in a hurry.*

"Any excitement on the cattle drive?" Brynna asked.

Sam told her stepmother about seeing Tinkerbell and Teddy Bear, Katie Sterling, Mr. Martinez, and Duke Fairchild.

"What about that wild horse?" Lynn asked.

"Wild horse?" Brynna asked. Her tone sharpened a bit, since the welfare of wild horses was her business.

Sam blinked. She and Jen had ridden out alone this morning when they saw the Phantom.

"You know," Lynn said, sounding frustrated. "The blond one?"

"Oh! The mare that followed us in!" Sam said. "She's not wild."

"Well, she wasn't wearing any kind of"—Lynn's hands gestured around her own head—"leather getup for riding."

Sam laughed. "She's a stray," she told Brynna. "A really beautiful—"

"I'm going to be sick," Diana blurted.

Her face had gone milk white, and she weaving, trying to keep her balance.

Dr. Yung was simultaneously steadying her, reaching for a plastic basin and saying, "We're going to need a little privacy here . . . and Brynna? Could you do me a favor and phone for an ambulance?"

Chapter Seven ∾

$\mathcal{L}$inc Slocum crowded to the front of those gathered outside the first aid station as Diana was loaded into the back of the ambulance.

Sam figured it was paranoid to think he was glaring at her. Still, she wished he'd been someplace else as Brynna snatched her keys out of her pocket and rattled off instructions.

"I'm sure I'll talk with Wyatt before you do, but if by some chance I can't reach him before he picks you up, tell him why I was so late to work and where I'm going, okay?"

"I will," Sam said. She hesitated before she added, "I was going to try to call him and tell him not to come until later. Do you think he'd mind? Mr. Ryden wants us—me and Jen—to be his guests at the first performance of the rodeo tonight."

"Wow," Brynna said. She frowned after the ambulance as it drove off. "You ask, and if he hesitates, just tell him I'll come back into town for you."

"Okay," Sam said slowly, but she was pretty sure the rodeo ended late.

After all, there'd be fireworks, courtesy of Linc Slocum.

Sam tried not to glance at him. She would have been successful, too, if he hadn't given a snort. She and Brynna both looked, and caught him glaring after Lynn Cooper as she waved good-bye and hustled off to work.

It figured that Linc Slocum wouldn't like reporters, Sam thought. Rumor said Linc Slocum had a shady past. He probably wouldn't like seeing the truth in print.

"I'd really better get going if I'm going to be there to help her check into the hospital," Brynna said. "She won't feel like filling out all those forms."

When Brynna covered her mouth against a yawn, Sam couldn't help admiring her stepmother. Tired as she was, Brynna had not only found medical care for a reluctant stranger; now she wanted to be beside her to help her with paperwork.

Sam knew she shouldn't force Brynna to make two round trips between the ranch and Darton in one day. In the last few weeks, she'd bet her stepmother had taken a hundred naps. Every time she sat still, her eyelids drooped and she fell asleep.

"Do you have to go with her?" Sam asked. Surely there were people at the hospital to help Diana McKenzie.

"I think I should," Brynna said, shifting her keys in her hand. "I'm trying to get her to call her parents, but she's not going for it."

"Just do it," Sam said. Brynna rarely had qualms about getting involved when the welfare of kids was concerned. "It's for her own good."

Sam bit her lip after the words escaped. She sounded like Gram!

Brynna smiled. "I would, but Diana's over eighteen years old. That makes her a legal adult and in charge of her own medical decisions."

"I bet you'll talk her into it," Sam said. Brynna could be pretty convincing.

"I'll try," Brynna said. "And don't worry about wearing me out," she added. "Tomorrow's Saturday and I can sleep in. I wouldn't want you to miss this rodeo."

Brynna kissed Sam on the cheek and left.

When Sam looked around for Linc, he was gone and she was glad.

She shouldn't be surprised, Sam told herself as she walked in what she hoped was the direction of the barn. Linc didn't like to be thought a bully, so he rarely said anything to her in front of other adults.

He'd slipped up once today. When Linc had grumbled that remark about her being unwelcome, he hadn't expected Hal Ryden to hear. Whatever was bothering him, Linc wasn't likely to blame it on her again. At least not in front of Brynna.

If she knew Linc, he'd gone home. The fairgrounds baked under the late-afternoon sun, and though there was an atmosphere of excitement preceding this first rodeo performance, he'd be happier in his air-conditioned mansion.

With the barns in sight, Sam took a shortcut between two high-sided corrals. She had to hurry. She'd been gone so long that she wouldn't blame Jen for leaving without her. After all, they were both curious to learn more about the beautiful chocolate mare.

Sam caught a whiff of cigarette smoke. She'd seen signs warning against smoking in the barn or grandstand areas. She couldn't imagine the rules would be much different over here, where the bucking cattle were confined with bales of flammable hay.

People who had permission to be here, behind the scenes, probably wouldn't be so careless. The smoke must have blown to her from the carnival area.

Despite her hurry, Sam paused to stare at a pen of Brahma bulls. Three clustered around a plastic water bucket hanging on the side of their corral, while others dozed.

"Well if it's not Miss Stick-her-nose-in-where-it-don't-belong." Linc Slocum stepped into her path, holding a cigarette. "I think I'll walk with you a piece and give you a little friendly advice."

"Thanks, but I'm in kind of a hurry," Sam said as she kept walking.

"Oh now, don't tell me you have something better to do than spy on people," he sneered.

She could sprint away from him, Sam thought. Linc's pumpkin-shaped body looked unsteady in his stylish boots.

Sam didn't run. She couldn't let him think he'd scared her off, but he must have seen her consider the idea.

"I was just joshin'," he said in a too-sweet tone. "But I did see the way you were sizing up that girl they put into the ambulance."

"What are you talking about? I was not," Sam snapped.

"'Course you were. It's a hobby with you, girl. You've just gotta know other folks' business."

Sam shook her head, focused on the barns, and Ace's bay head hanging over one of the stall doors.

Linc was nuts. She didn't spy on people. She never had, except maybe on Dad and Brynna before they got married, but she'd been younger then.

Sam took a quick turn between two corrals. One held two big Brangus-looking cows and calves and had a sign that read, BORN TO BUCK.

She heard Linc's boots scuff on the dirt. He was still behind her.

Where was everyone else? Shouldn't someone be getting the animals ready for the show?

"I kinda understood you diggin' into my background so I couldn't have that mustang stallion, but then you cozied up to old lady Allen and talked her into opening that wild horse sanctuary by telling her all about my plans for building a resort on her cattle ranch."

"She'd already made up her mind," Sam said. "Besides, I was only telling her the truth."

"I'm sure that truth's gonna be a real comfort to her. She could have been a millionaire if she'd sold that ranch, instead of worrying over a bunch of useless animals, wasting money that could keep her safe and comfortable in her old age."

This was no lie, Sam thought. Mrs. Allen's ranch land bordered some of Slocum's and he would have paid plenty for it.

Taking her silence as victory, Slocum quit pretending he was actually concerned. "You won't feel like such hot stuff when that old lady's in the poorhouse," he called after her.

She should have kept walking, but she didn't. Sam stopped, hands on hips, and turned to face him.

"Mr. Slocum, don't talk to me anymore, please. I don't know why you're so mad, but—"

She'd given him time to catch up. He was only a few feet away when he said, "Aren't you listenin', girl? You're ruining my reputation. I want to be on the board of the rodeo association, and reputation counts."

Linc slammed his fist into his opposite palm and the action must have shown him how crazy he was acting, because his expression turned sad.

"Look at what you've done to Ryan," Linc said sorrowfully. "Caused him three brushes with the police."

"What?" Sam's voice soared.

Ryan Slocum, Linc's son, had only been in Nevada a few months since leaving England, where he'd lived with his mother.

"First you told the sheriff about the Kenworthy palomino," Linc said quietly. "Then there was that hermit on the mountain you got Ryan involved with, and that whole uproar over our colt."

Our colt. Sam didn't remind Linc he'd promised Shy Boots, the colt his Appaloosa mare Hotspot had foaled, to her. And she'd had nothing to do with Ryan arranging Shy Boots' disappearance. Ryan had done it because he thought Linc was going to have the colt destroyed.

Linc could blame himself for forming such bad relationships with his children. She didn't feel a bit sorry for him, but she couldn't imagine how to put her feelings into words that were even half polite.

Luckily, she didn't have to do it.

"Sam!" Jen shouted as she jogged toward Sam. Jen's face was flushed from the heat and her blond braids bounced.

Jen to the rescue, Sam thought. She laughed out loud in relief. Leaving Linc Slocum behind, Sam walked determinedly toward her friend.

Chapter Eight ❧

"What did *he* want?" Jen asked. As they jogged side by side toward the arena, Jen held up crossed fingers. "Maybe he was the reason you had to go to the first aid station? I hope."

Sometimes Sam scolded Jen for her sarcasm. Not today.

"No such luck," Sam said. "He wanted to tell me I was giving him a bad reputation."

Jen stopped so suddenly that Sam jogged on past her.

"What?" Jen yelped. "*You're* giving *him*—" Jen beat the air with both hands, as if the air were full of bees, and her cheeks turned red. "Is he insane? Oh yeah, I forgot. Of course he is, but I can't believe he actually convinced someone to call you on the loudspeaker for that slice of baloney!"

Sam laughed until Jen's anger faded into a smile.

"You are the best friend," Sam said, and as she did, she realized she really should talk with Jen about the offer to buy Ace.

"Yes, I am *the* best friend. One of a kind, thank goodness," Jen bragged. "If there were two of us, we'd take that jerk down for you."

"Someday," Sam promised, and then she gave Jen a good-natured shove to keep moving. There was no time to talk seriously right now. "But it wasn't him paging me. It was Brynna. She's the one who picked up the girl who rolled her truck."

"Wow," Jen said. "Living proof a biologist can be brave. I guess I'll have to be a mathematician."

"Jen! You're brave. You were just offering to beat up Linc."

"Only if I had a clone."

They were almost to the arena when Hal Ryden came striding toward them.

On the trail, he'd seemed mostly cowboy. Now he had the manner of the businessman he was.

"Girls, the rodeo vet's willing to take a look at that mare, but he's on a dead run. The standards are tight for watching over the stock and he's not quite sure when he'll get to the arena to check her over. Since my guys need to get ready for the show —"

"We can hang out with the mare until the vet gets there," Sam finished.

She couldn't wait to get a closer look at the mare and try to start unraveling her mystery.

"Atta girl," Hal said. He gave her a pat on the back that was more suitable for a horse, but Sam stayed on her feet as Hal continued. "Feel free to stick her in one of my stalls. That's if he gives her a clean bill of health."

"I guess no one's reported her missing?" Jen asked.

"Haven't had a chance to check. If I were missing a horse, though, I'm not sure I'd call the rodeo grounds."

"Maybe the sheriff," Sam mused.

"Might be the vet can help you puzzle that out," Hal said. "As for me, I've got flag girls to line up, pickup men to check with, and a whole load of broncs and bulls to pamper." He'd taken two steps away before he turned back. "Almost forgot," he said, pulling two tickets from his pocket. "These are for you. Best seats in the house. You'll be right over the chutes, so you can watch the riders mount up."

"Thank you so much," Sam said, then she elbowed Jen, who was staring at Hal with something like hero worship.

"Thank you," Jen said.

Hal Ryden touched the brim of his hat in farewell.

❋ ❋ ❋

The mare wore a borrowed rope halter and she was tied just outside the arena where a dozen furled and colorful flags leaned against a fence, waiting to be carried in during the grand entry.

Ears pricked to catch the sounds of activity all around her, the mare looked curious but not nervous. She stretched toward the knot in the lead rope, tying her to a ring, and lipped it experimentally.

"Hey, beauty, you're not going anywhere," Jen said as they approached.

The mare switched her white-gold tail and stamped, seeming only a little disappointed that her escape plan had failed.

"She really is pretty," Sam said.

"Not a bit spooky, either," Jen added.

The mare's wide, gentle eyes and nicker said she thought they'd brought treats.

"What have I got for you, pretty girl?" Jen mused, digging into her pocket. "Just crumbs from the bribe I had to give to my own horse. That's despicable, isn't it?"

Together Sam and Jen studied the mare, then skimmed their hands over her coat.

"Dusty, but not dirty," Sam observed. "And I only see one knot in her mane."

"She hasn't been on the run for long," Jen said. "And since she jilted the great Phantom, she can't be very lonely."

Jen's teasing had a little too much bite to it to be funny,

Sam thought. Or maybe she was just feeling sensitive because of Linc's accusations.

"Am I nosy?" Sam asked suddenly.

Jen drew a long breath. Her hands paused on the mare and she regarded Sam with an analytical look. "Define 'nosy.'"

"I guess that answers my question," Sam said in a joking tone. She wove her fingers through the mare's mane and worked to undo that single knot, trying not to pout over Linc being right.

"I'd say you're curious," Jen said, "but most intelligent people are, and you're sure not one of those girls who listens to every conversation, ready to memorize any gossip she can recycle for an audience. Like, when my parents were having problems, you didn't pump me for details—"

"Of course not!" Sam said.

"See? And the HARP girls, well, because they're 'at risk,' there's lots of rumors you could spread about them, but you're uncomfortable knowing what you're supposed to know about them. You don't go digging for more. I don't call that nosy. Who said you were?"

"Nobody," Sam said, but she didn't expect Jen to believe her for an instant.

"Slocum, right?" Jen guessed.

Sam was nodding when the vet arrived.

"Is this our runaway?" A short, fit man in a white straw hat and jeans bustled up, hands outstretched to examine the mare even before the rest of his body caught up.

His conversation seemed to be aimed more at soothing the horse than drawing information from Sam and Jen.

"Haven't finished looking at the stock just in from the drive," he said, coaxing the mare's mouth open. "Usually it's easier on them than trucking, though. With trucks, sometimes you'll be driving along and a car pulls in front of you and wham! You've gotta slam on the brakes. Teeth okay," he said and began lifting the mare's feet for inspection. "Then, what happens when you get mothers and calves in two different trucks?"

Sam was wondering if the vet expected an answer, when he went on.

"You finally arrive at your destination, the pairs don't 'mother up,' that's what, and bingo! You got a leppy calf on your hands."

"Right," Jen began.

The vet looked up from the hoof he was examining and frowned at her, so she didn't finish.

"Hal tells me you were with the drive. No accidents you saw? Hello?" He'd released the last hoof and stood looking at them, arms folded over his belt.

"No," Sam blurted. "Nothing went wrong with the cattle that I saw."

"I—" Jen started to say something, but the vet

held up an index finger, then put one arm over the mare's back and bent with the stethoscope to listen to her heart.

"Okay, sounds good," he murmured. Then, with his eyes unfocused, he began feeling the mare's skin for lumps and bumps.

"Took a tumble, did you, girl?"

Sam and Jen looked at each other, but this time they had to answer.

"It must have happened before she joined up with us," Sam said, but the vet didn't seem to hear.

"Want to trot her away from me?" The vet jerked the lead rope loose and handed it to Jen. She jogged the mare and the vet watched. "No stiffness or lameness. That's good. And the shape she's in, I'll bet she's had her vaccinations."

"She fell?" Jen asked once she'd brought the mare back to him.

"Yeah, whether you saw it or not, she's got some bumps and scuffs consistent with a pretty good fall. Nothing that needs treatment, really, beyond washing up. You'll take care of that, won't you?"

"Sure," Sam said, but her mind raced ahead. They'd be watching the rodeo and then they'd be leaving. She'd have to ask Hal who should care for the horse. But he was already doing the mare a favor, giving her a place to stay. Sam sawed her teeth over her bottom lip. What became of lost horses? Did Sheriff Ballard have a place to board them temporarily?

"Got a saddle bronc mare—Dixie Chick, know her?—that got her head through a fence reaching for who knows what and laid her neck wide open. Since she'd already been drawn for the event, Hal's gotta—"

The vet broke off as the mare nuzzled his pocket. "Nothing for you, girl," he said kindly.

That was twice she'd gone looking for treats, Sam thought. Maybe she was hungry.

"No one's turned up claiming this horse, am I right?" the vet said, giving her a clap on the shoulder as if he really had to be going.

"Right," Jen said. She looked a little dizzy from keeping up with the vet's talk.

"They will," he said, shoving his stethoscope farther down into his medical bag.

What if there's a reward offered for her? Sam's mind spun with possibilities. Of course she couldn't collect all of it, but maybe she, Jen, and Hal could share the reward. Maybe a little extra cash would ease her guilt over not selling Ace.

"She's gentle and sweet," the vet said as he buckled his bag closed, gaze still on the mare. "Easy to handle and she's got a chip. I'd say she's been in competition—this wide-open arena and all the activity doesn't bother her. She's no youngster, though. Twelve to fourteen, I'd say. Maybe somebody's broodmare."

"What is she?" Jen asked.

"Which breed, you mean? I was afraid you'd ask." The vet blew through his lips. "I'm really more of a cattle specialist. Give me a rank bull out of Nobody, by WhotheHeckKnows, and I can figure out his great auntie, but this mare . . . ," he said, shaking his head. "I'll tell you, the only horse I've seen that reminds me of this one was ridden by an old-time movie star. Can't remember his name, but the horse was called Coco. Darned if I can remember its bloodlines. If I ever knew."

With a final pat, the vet stepped away. Sam thought he already had one boot pointed toward his next assignment when he said, "I'd like to take another look at her eyes when I have time. It's no emergency, no injury, but something's not quite right. Tell Hal she's got as clean a bill of health as I can give her without running blood work. He can put her in with his stock without a second thought, I'd say."

For the first time it occurred to Sam that Hal Ryden had risked a lot by being neighborly and allowing them to stable their horses with his. Horses carried all kinds of equine illnesses.

Silly, Ace, or this stray mare could endanger the livestock that earned Hal's living. A contagious disease, even if it wasn't serious, could cost him a performance or even an entire rodeo season, and that would mean the loss of thousands of dollars.

Once the vet had vanished, the girls took turns leading the mare to the barn. As showtime drew near, the rodeo grounds were an obstacle course. The bulls that had been eating alfalfa or resting on the ground with folded legs, stood up. They ignored their salt licks and flapped their ears at the music from the arena.

The chocolate mare noticed the little tractors rolling from place to place carrying people in a hurry or towing trailers full of cedar shavings for clean bedding. She noticed, but didn't seem to care.

"She's bomb-proof," Jen said when a girl leading four sheep—for the mutton-busting competition, Jen explained—darted in front of them. "Too bad she's not a mustang. HARP could use a horse like this."

HARP—*or a therapy horse program*, Sam thought suddenly. That would be even better than earning a reward.

Sam's heart thudded so hard, she was amazed Jen didn't hear it.

What if no owner surfaced for this horse? She'd been wandering in the mountains, after all. It would be a mercy to take her in and use her with disabled riders, wouldn't it?

Buying her might be a problem, except . . .

If she had no owner, maybe the sheriff would

just say she was free to a good home. Wasn't that possible?

Suddenly Sam realized Jen's fingers were snapping in front of her face.

"Huh?"

"That's not exactly the articulate response I've come to expect from my friend who gets A's in English and journalism," Jen told her. "What I was saying was, once we clean her up, let's take a quick run through the events center. Last year they had everything a cowgirl could want."

Sam and Jen found a stock-washing stall near the barns. Since it was almost time for the rodeo to begin, it was vacant.

"Who's getting wet?" Jen asked playfully, lifting the hand shower off its hook and squirting it toward Sam.

She danced out of the way. If they were staying at the rodeo until long after dark, she didn't want soggy boots.

"How about if we just tie her in there?" Sam asked, but just then the mare gave her back pocket a nudge. "Hey!"

The mare was probably still looking for treats, but her exploration forced Sam to step in a puddle of standing water that had been left over from the last shower.

"Good choice, girl," Jen told the horse.

So, since Sam was already wet, she stood in the washing stall, formed of two cinder-block walls that made a corner, and let Jen spray the mare clean.

Delighted by the cooling spray, the mare wiggled her ears, then shook like a big dog. Soaked, Sam still couldn't get mad at the horse.

Back in the barn, Jen borrowed grooming tools without a qualm, and they set to work. They were burnishing the mare's chocolate coat when Lynn Cooper came back with her cameraman.

"She looks great," Lynn said. Then, as if she'd remembered she was afraid of horses, she added, "Has she bitten or kicked either of you?"

"Nope, she's sweet as pie," Sam assured the reporter.

"Are you sure she didn't buck you into a water trough or something?" Lynn asked, looking at the drips still falling from Sam's clothing.

"It wasn't exactly her fault," Sam said.

"Well, I brought her a treat so that she wouldn't do something ugly to me. I saw it in the cowgirl mall," Lynn said, gesturing toward the events center. "And it even looked delicious to me. I've got it in my purse, but first, I want to get your reaction to something." Lynn's eyes took in both girls. "What do you think of doing a short TV piece on this mystery mare?"

"Great idea," Jen said. "Someone's bound to recognize her."

"It's a great story, too," Sam said. Her mind veered back to the idea of being a photojournalist. "She's photogenic. She came out of nowhere and joined up with the herd." Sam nodded.

"I'd stay in the living room to watch the news if a story like that came on," Jen said.

"And tune in for more details the next night, I bet," Sam teased.

Then she saw Lynn watching her with a calculating look.

"What?" Sam said.

"Nothing bad," Lynn assured her. "I don't know much about horses, and you told me last year, when we did that earthquake story, that you were on the school newspaper. Isn't that right?"

"Yeah," Sam said slowly.

"What would you think of working with me for a couple days this week on this horse's story?"

Sam didn't know what to say, but when she noticed the mare posing for the cameraman who seemed to go everywhere with Lynn, she smiled.

"You mean investigative reporting?" Jen said. Then she elbowed Sam. "You've done that before. I mean, that picture you took of that stallion stealing mares when everyone else thought it was the Phantom. That was investigative reporting."

Jen was always trying to push her. Sam thought about Ace and his comfort zone. The little mustang wasn't happy off the ranch and range. She wasn't sure she could do something like this.

"I don't know," Sam said. "You wouldn't have to know much about horses to do this story, Lynn."

"Sam, why not?" Jen said.

"Did you forget the part where this is a real television station?" Sam asked, but part of her brain was thinking how cool it would be to help track down the mare's story.

"It wouldn't be official," Lynn said. "We'd just put our heads together once or twice."

"Sam," Jen said in a wheedling tone.

"Would you like to help?" Lynn asked.

"Oh no," Jen said, shaking her head. "Come see me when you need statistics. The only reason I pass English is because I've put together a writing formula my teachers haven't caught on to yet."

"It'll be strictly for fun. I just think you have the instincts to help get this horse home," Lynn said, smiling. "It's what my old journalism professor called a nose for news."

Sam gave a short laugh. "Yeah, someone just told me an hour ago that I was nosy."

"That's not the same thing at all," Lynn said, and then she gasped.

The chocolate mare's head shot out toward Lynn. The horse dusted her lips over the reporter's neck and down to her purse. Lynn stood stiff and still as a tree trunk.

"She's looking for a place to bite me," Lynn said with grim conviction.

"I doubt it," Sam said. "I think she smells that treat you brought."

The mare bumped her nose against the purse. She did it so hard, her forelock flopped up, then down.

Lynn took a step back as she fumbled with her purse.

The mare crowded forward.

"You're going to have to give me room to get it," Lynn said. Eyes full of surprise, she glanced up at Sam. "Her mouth is kind of soft, except for the whiskers."

"Uh-huh," Sam and Jen said together.

Moving quickly, Lynn ripped the cellophane off the oats-and-honey treat.

"Okay, no horse spit," Lynn warned the mare.

"Hand flat," Sam ordered. "*Totally* flat."

She didn't want to tell Lynn that the mare's teeth could accidentally bite through a finger as easily as they'd snap that cookie in two.

With the cookie in sight, the mare's left front leg bent at the knee.

"What's she doing?" Jen wondered.

Slowly, the mare knelt with her right leg extended.

It was a graceful and pretty trick, especially when she arched her neck and bobbed her head so that her forelock veiled her eyes and brushed the ground.

"She's bowing," Lynn said incredulously.

Then, before she could turn to him, the cameraman said, "I've got it."

"Someone's going to see this and know her," Jen insisted.

Sam agreed. Who wouldn't recognize a chocolate-and-cream horse with such good manners?

Chapter Nine

"*I*t has to be just window shopping, because I don't have any money," Jen said.

Sam kissed Ace on the nose and told him good-bye before the girls headed toward what Lynn had called "the cowgirl mall" in the events center.

"Dad gave me this for expenses," Sam said, pulling the bill partway out of her jeans pocket. "And I'll share."

"Things are awfully expensive here," Jen grumbled. "But that ought to just about cover two sodas and two corn dogs. Thanks."

Sam shot a last look down the row of stall doors. Three pairs of dark-brown eyes in palomino, bay, and chocolate faces watched her.

"Don't you feel just a little weird about leaving Silly and Ace in unfamiliar stalls?" Sam asked.

"This place has better safety standards than home," Jen said. "And look, the lights are on in the center hall between the stalls, so they can look in and see their neighbors. I refuse to feel guilty. Let's go."

First, they stopped at a telephone booth and called River Bend Ranch.

When she talked with Gram, Sam discovered that Brynna had already called Dad. He planned to pick them up after the rodeo, with a trailer for Ace and Silly, at ten o'clock.

Delighted by the night of freedom, Sam shot a clenched fist toward the evening sky and still kept her grip on the phone.

"Samantha," Gram cautioned as though she could see the small celebration. "If you're not waiting for him at Gate C at ten on the dot, I can't be responsible for what happens to the rest of your summer."

"Jen and I will be there, Gram, with both horses ready to load," she said. Then, just before she hung up, Sam added, "I promise."

On their own and giddy, Sam and Jen clambered up the wide concrete stairs to the top of the events center and arrived breathless. A gabble of voices surrounded them. Colorful and crowded booths, full of wonderful things they couldn't afford, encircled the top story and overlooked a small arena.

The soft plop of hooves came from down below. Loping in figure-eights, sliding to controlled stops, horses warmed up for the rodeo's opening performance. Almost all the riders were female.

With spangled shirts and long hair streaming from under new cowgirl hats, they would look high-spirited and pretty when they rode in front of the grandstands. Right now, though, the queen candidates, barrel racers, and flag girls concentrated. They rode with skillful grace, working the nerves out of horses that would perform in front of a huge audience tonight.

Breathing in the smell of new leather, Sam and Jen stared at hand-tooled saddles, headstalls, and belts in the first booth.

"Oh, look." Jen grabbed Sam's arm and dragged her toward a display of glittering silver jewelry shaped like horses, stars, and coyotes.

"But look at that." Sam pointed to a rack of scarves, skirts, and T-shirts fringed with suede and glass beads.

In every booth they filled out cards for contests and drawings, even when it seemed silly.

"What are you going to do with—" Jen broke off to read the entry blank Sam was writing on. "'A rope made of weighted nylon in neon colors specially made to be visible in the dark'? Sam, if I roped like you—"

"Hush now," said the booth's attendant. Not much older than they were, the guy wore a cowboy hat and sat astride a saddle on a stand. He spun one of the ropes in a perfect loop without even looking at it. "Pretty girls like you must have sweethearts that'd love one of these."

"Of course we do," Jen said seriously. "We just haven't met them yet."

Trying not to giggle, Sam grabbed Jen's arm and towed her to the next display. By the time they were ready to leave, they'd entered drawings for a silver mounted saddle, rainbow saddle blanket, twenty pounds of beef jerky, and a truck.

"That popcorn smells really good," Sam said as they passed by a snack bar. "We never ate lunch you know. I'm hungry."

"Me, too, but I hear those corn dogs calling my name."

"I think I hear them, too, and they're over in the carnival," Sam said.

With thirty minutes left before the rodeo's grand entry, they headed toward the two acres of rides and junk food. There was no time to ride the Tilt-A-Whirl, Octopus, or bucking bull, but they could look.

Balloons popped and coins clinked as people threw darts and tossed quarters, trying to win huge stuffed animals.

"Can you imagine the expression on your dad's face

if we showed up at ten o'clock with both horses and one of those?" Jen mused as she stared after a guy who'd just won a purple bunny the size of a grizzly bear.

"He might take the horses home," Sam said, "but he'd definitely leave us and our bunny behind."

Looking for dinner, they passed up garlic fries and cotton candy for corn dogs and jumbo cups of freshly squeezed lemonade. By the time Jen had squirted a neat line of ketchup on her corn dog and Sam had painted hers with mustard, it was time to dig their rodeo tickets from their pockets and stand in line.

Sam sighed in contentment.

The day's heat had faded under a cool breeze. She had a fun evening ahead with her best friend. Ace was safe in a cozy stall, and after he'd acted up today, she could reasonably put off thoughts of selling him. Maybe Amelia's grandmother would never call.

She even knew the Phantom was all right. Sure, he'd been snubbed by the chocolate mare, and he'd kept his distance from Sam and Jen, but he'd shown no ill effects from the explosion that had robbed him of his hearing just two weeks ago.

The Ferris wheel turned to tinkling music, flashing its red, yellow, green, and orange lights against a lavender sky.

"It's a perfect summer night," Sam said as she clomped across the wooden deck toward their lofty seats.

"You had to say that, didn't you?" Jen muttered. "What's wrong with—"

Sam stopped. She looked down at the number on her ticket and up again. This couldn't be right.

"Just perfect," Jen said in a sarcastic tone. "We're sitting directly in front of Linc Slocum and all his new friends."

It turned out that Linc didn't want to talk with them any more than Sam and Jen wanted to talk with him. They were restless and aware of him, and worried about the empty seat beside Sam, until the bareback bronc riding started. Then they forgot everything else.

From the minute the horse in the chute below them started kicking, ready to escape her confinement and the rider on her back, Sam couldn't look away.

This was the event Jake had said his brother Kit competed in. As Sam looked down at the young men mounting the horses in the chute below them, she could see why he found it so exciting.

The rodeo announcer explained that bareback bronc riding was the most physically demanding of all the rodeo events. Suddenly, Sam saw why.

"Oh my gosh! They don't have a saddle or reins or anything except that little thing that looks like a suitcase handle."

"It's called a rigging," Jen said. "But you're right. It's the only thing they can touch. Even when their free arm is flying around like that," Jen said, pointing. "It can't touch the horse, rigging, or even the cowboy's hat, or they're disqualified."

Sam grabbed her right hand with her left and grimaced. What would happen to the delicate bones inside if her body were slamming back, away from her fingers, while she tried to hang onto hundreds of pounds of plunging horse?

"I admire their riding," Sam said, "but I still don't like the way they spur the horses. And that bucking strap—"

"Flank strap," Jen corrected. "And weren't you listening to the announcer? Those horses are trained athletes. They're worth thousands of dollars, and cowboys can be thrown out of the rodeo if they do anything to hurt horses or bulls."

"I heard him," Sam said, and though she enjoyed watching the explosive contest between the men and horses, she still hadn't made up her mind as to what she really thought about it.

She did smile each time a pickup man swooped in and placed each rider safely on the ground.

"I can see Jake doing that," Sam said. Jen nodded, but her eyes didn't leave the action in the arena.

Overly protective Jake would be great at riding to the rescue, Sam thought, *but he'd probably want to ride broncs like Kit.*

Jake never wanted to talk about Kit, so she didn't know much about him—just that he was the oldest Ely brother and Jake was the youngest. Kit had left home when Jake was a little boy and rarely returned unless he was badly injured.

Halfway into the next event, saddle bronc riding, Linc's voice boomed out. He sat directly behind Sam, and she could tell he was trying to sound like a real cowboy.

"Why, I been out in the desert so long, I know all the lizards by their first names," Linc chuckled. Alone.

Sam cringed. He'd told that joke earlier today, and it hadn't been very funny the first time.

Most of the laughter during the events was for the rodeo announcer, who joked while he narrated the events.

"Son, I'm afraid you tied your hand onto somethin' the rest of you can't ride," he said to the bronc rider who was flying off a horse named Volcano. "C'mon, now, folks. Your applause is all the reward this cowboy's gonna get."

The announcer recited a list of rodeo superstitions, too. Even Jen had never heard that rodeo riders always shaved before a performance, but they never wore yellow because it was rumored to drain away bravery. They never put their cowboy hats on a bed, but sometimes they wore different colored socks on each foot for luck.

The calf roping event was underway when Lynn Cooper, without her cameraman, slipped into the empty seat beside Sam.

"How're you two liking the show?" she leaned over to ask in a low voice.

"Great!" they responded together.

"I just watched our mystery mare piece on the TV in the media trailer, and it wasn't bad," Lynn said modestly. "The station kept the footage of you two riding in with the herd, but cut away just before your horse lost it."

"It was my fault—" Sam began, but Lynn brushed away her apology.

"You two looked mighty impressive!" the reporter said, then held out her hand. Sam and Jen took turns slapping it in congratulations, as a clown with two dogs wearing ruffled collars performed in the arena.

Jen's laughter blended in with that of those watching the clown and Sam guessed that was why Lynn picked that moment to ask, "If you were investigating that mystery horse, where would you start?"

Lynn couldn't have guessed the laughter around them would stop so abruptly, or that her last few words would fall into the suddenly quiet air.

Worse than that, Lynn couldn't have guessed Linc Slocum would care about any investigation involving Sam.

But Sam realized he cared a lot when Linc pretended to drop something between his boots. Then he leaned forward and, speaking so softly no one else heard, muttered,

"Don't forget: Curiosity killed the cat."

Chapter Ten

*I*t's a joke, Sam tried to tell herself. A cliché, even.

"Curiosity killed the cat," Gram had said just a few days ago when Dad opened the oven to look at a baking cake and burned his finger.

When Linc Slocum said it, though, Sam got chills.

And now Jen was answering Lynn's question, without knowing what Linc had muttered.

"What we did when Shy Boots was missing—" Jen paused and looked at Sam, expecting her to join in.

Sam flashed Jen a look to be quiet, hoping she didn't have to give her a kick to back it up. While Jen was trying to puzzle out Sam's frown, Lynn made things even worse.

"Who's Shy Boots?" she asked.

Finally Jen got Sam's hint.

Jen glanced back at Linc Slocum and smiled. Jen knew Linc would be able to hear. She was just including him so he wouldn't think they were gossiping.

"Shy Boots is a darling Appaloosa colt and his mother is Hotspot," Jen told Lynn. "Hotspot belongs to Gold Dust Ranch and they were both stolen."

Boots shuffled behind Sam. One of the men sitting with Linc tried to get a look at his face as he asked, "Is that so, Linc?"

Linc cleared his throat, stalling. Sam saw Jen's eyes blink thoughtfully behind her glasses.

Oh, no. Jen's logical mind was reconsidering her choice of words. Technically, Ryan, Linc's son, had hidden the two horses from his father because Linc wanted to get rid of the "mongrel" foal. Later, the foal had been stolen.

"Actually—" Jen began, pushing her glasses up her nose.

"Actually," Sam cut in, "we already have a huge, gigantic, mega advantage over last time, when we were trying to find those horses," Sam sputtered. "Because the mare's been on television!"

Jen raised her eyebrows, and her mouth twisted in a mocking grin. Even though Sam were really overdoing it, Jen went along.

"Right," Jen said. "I bet someone's already called your station. With that mare's distinctive coloring and that trick, someone's sure to recognize her."

"So, you're thinking," Lynn said in a considering tone, "that the horse jumped out of someone's pasture?"

"Maybe," Jen said, giving a one-shouldered shrug. "Plus, fence posts rot, wire sags, and now and then someone leaves a gate open."

All those ideas made sense, Sam thought as music revved up the audience for the next event. But Jen's mention of horse thieves had given Sam an idea.

While Jen told Lynn how they'd distributed flyers and checked the Internet for the missing foal, Sam decided there *could* be another explanation for a well-groomed, well-fed mare to turn up in the Pinion Pine mountains.

What if she'd been stolen?

What if the thief had been bringing her to someone who collected exotic livestock?

What if the thief was Karl Mannix and, stopping to water or exercise the mare, the thief had accidentally lost her, just as he had Hotspot?

Staring without seeing, Sam focused on the arena. Steer wrestling had begun and the announcer was attributing a missed catch to "steer snot."

Jen heard that much, because she groaned in disgust.

Sam, however, was spinning a story that explained the mystery mare. It was improbable, maybe even far-fetched, but Karl Mannix, who hadn't yet been arrested for the theft of Hotspot and Shy Boots, could have stolen this mare elsewhere and decided to return to Gold Dust Ranch where he was sure of a sale to a man with more money than morals.

If he'd still been driving the Hummer, the arrest would have been a piece of cake, since Sheriff Ballard had made casts of the tire tracks. But a vintage Scout had been towing the trailer that had—

Wait. A mental stop sign popped up in the middle of Sam's musing.

Diana—not Karl Mannix—had been driving the Scout.

And the trailer had been empty.

Sam shook her head.

How had she made that mental leap? She must be wearier than she'd thought. Sam glanced at her watch, then counted on her fingers. She'd been up for fifteen hours. That was why she'd jumped to a conclusion that made no sense.

"I'm going back to the studio to see if they've had any calls," Lynn said. She half stood, then reached across to shake Jen's hand. "It's been nice meeting you, Jennifer, and if I ever need help with statistics, I'll give you a call."

* * *

Since they didn't want to take a chance of being late meeting Sam's dad at Gate C, the girls slipped out of their grandstand seats before the fireworks began.

Linc's glare followed them. Sam felt it between her shoulder blades. Apparently Jen did, too.

"You know he's taking it personally that we're leaving before the fireworks he paid for," Jen muttered.

Sam nodded, but she didn't say anything until they'd left the grandstands and started toward the barns.

"He's already mad at us, but my Dad isn't," Sam said. "And he will be, if we're late getting the horses out to Gate C. I mean, this is kind of a big favor. Dad's usually asleep by ten o'clock and up again at four."

"My dad, too," Jen said as they walked past uniformed Girl Scouts who were picking up litter before the rodeo grounds closed for the night. "So Linc's whole 'you're ruining my reputation' thing is about wanting to be part of the Rodeo Association?" Jen asked.

"That's what he told me," Sam said. "You know, he needs to grow up." Sam looked around quickly to be sure she hadn't been overheard.

"He sure does," Jen said, sounding grim.

Sam knew she should be quiet. It was easy for her to be mad, but Linc Slocum's attitude was even harder for Jen to take. Linc was her dad's boss. Jen's family lived on Linc's ranch, and it had once been their own.

"Don't you think it's just like school?" Sam asked Jen. "He doesn't care about rodeo. He just wants to be part of the popular clique."

Ace's neigh rang out from the barns. Even before she could see him, Ace had heard her coming. *Or maybe smelled her,* Sam thought. It had been a long, dusty time since last night's shower.

"There's your pal," Jen said.

Sam smiled. She could always count on Ace to cheer her up.

They were almost at the barn when the fireworks ended.

Behind them, Sam heard parents urging cranky children toward the parking lot. Some car engines were already starting up.

"Looks like someone else came to see his horse," Sam said.

A single figure stood spotlighted by the barn lights. It was a guy, probably a little older than Jake. He wore khaki pants and a polo shirt. He looked very preppy and out of place.

"Uh-huh," Jen said, then she caught Sam's arm and stopped her. "Give him a minute. It sounds like he's getting all mushy with his horse, and you know he'd be embarrassed."

The guy held out his hand for the horse to sniff.

"Hey, lass, you remember me, don't you?"

Lass? Is that what he'd said?

Sam didn't shuffle her feet, but she leaned forward as if she could pick up his prattle to the horse more clearly. Then she recognized the horse.

"He's—" Sam began.

"Shh," Jen said, but she'd noticed, too.

He was standing outside the chocolate mare's stall.

Jen's shushing must have carried, because the guy turned toward them.

"Pretty horses," he called, moving down a stall to peer inside. "Are they yours?"

"A couple of them are," Jen shouted back.

Then they started walking again.

Sam felt disappointed. "Too bad. I thought her owner had shown up."

"Me, too," Jen said. "Didn't I hear him right? I thought he asked if she remembered him."

"I thought so, too," Sam said.

At the same moment, she and Jen lengthened their strides, but they were too late to ask the guy what he'd meant.

By the time they reached the pool of light, he'd already darted around the end of the barn and blended into the crowd of rodeogoers headed for home.

❖ ❖ ❖

After greeting their horses, who seemed quite at ease in their temporary homes, Sam and Jen began deciding whether they should ride Ace and Silly to Gate C instead of leading them.

"It's up to you," Jen said. "Which do you think will keep Ace calmer?"

"I don't know. He's never acted skittish before." Sam regarded the bay mustang. Head hanging over the stall door, he watched the crowd move past, then turned to her with ears trembling at the tips. He was asking a question, too.

"You'd have more control in the saddle," Jen mused.

"*You'd* have more control in the saddle," Sam said. "I'm not so sure about me. But I guess we could hope for that whole herd mentality thing and have him follow Silly."

"Yeah, and I think people are less likely to want to come up and pet him if you're riding him," Jen suggested.

While they saddled the horses, Sam worried about the chocolate mare.

She wasn't part of Hal's rodeo remuda, so who would take care of her? He probably had a groom come around and feed all the horses in the barn. And if there was an emergency, like a fire or an outbreak of a virus or something, they wouldn't leave her behind. Still, she was nobody's horse, and that was kind of sad.

Mounted up with ten minutes to spare, Sam and Jen started toward the gate.

Think like a horse, Sam told herself. *A scared horse.*

At first she thought Ace had recovered from his jitters. He didn't shy at a spinning pinwheel that was being brandished by toddler. He didn't mind the boy swinging his rolled rodeo program like a baseball bat. Ace didn't even notice the German shepherd in training as a companion dog. But when a water truck followed the crowd out of the rodeo grounds spraying a faint waterfall behind it to keep down the dust, Ace spotted it.

"You're not scared of that," Sam said confidently, but she shortened her reins and firmed her legs. "Would it scare you less if you could take a good long look at it? Or should I just hurry you on?"

Ace's ears flicked back to catch Sam's voice, but his choppy stride gave her no hints. So when Jen moved Silly into a quicker walk, Sam followed. It looked like the right decision.

Ace was almost past the truck when its waterfall shut off and some pump within the truck made a sound like a low, liquid groan.

Muscles flexed in the gelding's shoulder and his forelegs left the ground as he whirled away.

This time, Sam was ready for him. He'd veered

left, so she kept him turning in that direction until he'd made a complete circle. She and Ace were both taking short breaths by the time he was facing back in the original direction.

"Follow Silly's pretty white tail," Sam said. Even though her voice shook, she got the words out.

And Ace did just what she'd asked him to do.

They reached Gate C at 9:55. It was on the far side of the fairgrounds, and most of the cars were streaming out of Gates A and B.

Sam and Jen waited patiently. While the horses sniffed for weeds growing up through cracks in the asphalt, the girls stared wearily after red taillights that were streaming toward the town of Darton.

"Do you think someone around here owns her?" Sam said suddenly.

"The mare?" Jen asked. "I don't know, but it's only been a few hours since she was on television. Someone will turn up."

When Sam's sigh slipped out, Jen said, "She'll be fine. No one can ignore such a cool, well-mannered horse."

They lapsed into silence.

Could I fall asleep in the saddle? Sam wondered.

"It's ten fifteen," Jen said. She was staring at her watch—not annoyed, but just taken by surprise. "What do you think?"

Sam shook her head. The worry she'd been feeling

over Ace and the mare merged with this new concern.

"Dad's never late."

"This rodeo traffic is probably slowing him down," Jen said, but at ten thirty, when Dad still hadn't shown up, Sam knew something was wrong.

"What if I ride back to the phone booth and call?" Jen asked.

"Call who? My dad or your parents?"

"Either one," Jen said. "It's late, but if I know my mother, she's waiting up. Not only that; she will have calculated—down to the minute—how long it should take your dad to drive from here to Gold Dust Ranch. She'll freak out if I'm not home on time. Even if she's dozed off, I know she'd rather have me wake her up than sit there fretting."

"You're right," Sam said, but then both horses' heads flew up from snacking.

"We can quit worrying," Jen said as a truck pulling a Gold Dust Ranch stock trailer eased through the gate. "*My* dad's here."

Jen sounded relieved as her father drove past them and pulled over, but the sight of Jed Kenworthy instead of her own dad made Sam even more anxious.

The truck door opened and Jed jumped down, strong and thin, but his light-brown hair looked gray under the fairground lights and the droopy corners of his eyes made him look sad.

"My dad—"

"He's fine," Jed told Sam. His hand made a dismissing gesture as if whatever was wrong wasn't worth worrying about. "Let's get these horses loaded."

"But what's wrong?" Sam insisted.

Impatience flickered across Jed's sun-lined face. He was a tough man. When drought and low cattle prices had forced him to sell the Diamond K Ranch to Linc Slocum, he hadn't taken his money and fled the high desert. He'd stayed as foreman on the renamed Gold Dust Ranch, and Jed had never let Linc squash his "I'm the boss" attitude.

Now he expected her to do as she was told without explanation.

Well, I have a stubborn streak, too, Sam thought.

She stayed in the saddle, waiting, as Jen dismounted.

"Truck stalled," Jed told her.

"It does that all the time," Sam said, "and dad always gets it going again."

Jed gave a slight shake of his head, resigning himself to giving the whole story if he wanted her cooperation.

"Got to the middle of your bridge, engine died and wouldn't start again. Brynna's BLM truck's got no trailer hitch. Now come on down, Samantha, and maybe we'll get home before daybreak."

"Thanks for coming after us," Sam said as she

slipped from the saddle.

It wasn't quite an apology, but that was because she hadn't finished irritating Jed. She hadn't turned into a cooperative young lady, and she didn't want to get his hopes up.

Chapter Eleven ⁊

If animals could have instincts, why couldn't people have intuition?

Sam knew she wasn't just worried about the truck. Ever since she'd returned home from San Francisco, Dad's truck had suffered from breakdowns.

Sam fingered a lock of Ace's coarse black mane. New trucks cost money, and she was sitting astride a lot of it, but she wasn't just worried about money, either.

No, something else was gnawing at her. Her intuition insisted she'd missed some hint of trouble. She had to go back and check on the chocolate mare.

Jen and her dad were way too logical and level-headed to follow hunches, even hunches that wouldn't take no for an answer.

So Sam didn't try to explain.

"Sam?" Jen said as she finished loading Silly.

Jen was a good friend, as well as a perceptive one. She could read Sam's face as clearly as if Sam had handed her a note.

"You want to go back," Jen said flatly.

Sam nodded and Jen stepped aside, nodding toward her dad.

"I'm really sorry," Sam said to Jen's dad. "But I need to run back to the barn."

As Jed's astonished expression turned into a frown, Sam ground-tied Ace and edged a step away.

"I left something in the barn and I am so sorry. I'll race over there as fast as I can and load Ace the instant I get back —"

Jed snagged Ace's reins. "I'll get him in the trailer, but hurry. And I'm only doin' it 'cause you're wearin' your dad's stubborn look." Jed clucked his tongue and Ace followed him as Sam turned to go.

She heard Jed say, just loudly enough that she knew he meant for her to hear, "Jennifer, just remember what I told you: Only a fool argues with a skunk or a Forster whose mind is made up."

Sam ran as fast as her leather boots would allow.

The fairgrounds lay quiet around her. A paper cone from cotton candy blew across her path, dancing away in a late night breeze when she tried to pick it up.

Just before Sam reached the barn, she passed

Linc Slocum. Thumbs hooked through his belt loops, he stood with some other men. One was a rodeo security guard wearing a white shirt, fingers fiddling with the volume knob on his walkie-talkie.

Along with the other men, he was laughing a little too loudly. They acted like raucous boys instead of grown-ups. Sam guessed Linc Slocum had found his clique.

The barn was just yards away when Sam noticed the mare wasn't looking over the top half of her exterior door. Sam almost growled. There went her great idea of just giving the mare a pat on the neck and jetting back to the waiting Kenworthys.

Standing out here staring into the dark stall would probably be less productive than going through the end door and walking down the aisle until she reached the mare.

Hurry, Sam reminded herself, then jogged to the end and opened the door.

As she did, Sam caught the quick flash of light on an anxious equine eye.

But the gleam came from the fairgrounds lights outside. Illumination had followed her in as she opened the door. The stable lights, which had been on just half an hour ago when she and Jen had saddled up, were now out.

Still standing in the doorway, Sam breathed the comforting scent of cedar shavings and horses. She listened to the restless shifting of hooves.

If she were watching a movie, Sam knew she'd think the on-screen character was stupid to even consider going into the unfamiliar barn when she couldn't make out anything in the darkness.

But this was real life. She had no good reason to be scared.

The fairgrounds must have some master computer that doused the lights at ten o'clock.

Sam tried to remember what was inside the barn. A tack room on this end and a feed room down at the other end, with only an aisle down the middle and stalls on each side, right? There was no place for anyone to hide, unless they stretched out flat behind a hay bale or one of the costume trunks.

Sam put her hands on her hips and lifted her chin. If some creep had hidden inside one of the trunks, they'd give her a great head start with all the racket they'd have to make getting out.

"Hey, girl," Sam called out, feeling a little braver.

Two overlapping nickers and a snort came back and Sam almost smiled.

Her lips froze when she heard another sound. There, in the heartbeat of silence that followed the horses' greeting, she heard an indrawn human breath.

Maybe.

You're imagining it, Sam told herself.

She cleared her throat loudly.

If there was someone inside, it would be a member

of Hal's staff. But that didn't make sense. Anyone with a reason to be here would have long since called out to her.

No, it was just her and the horses.

And horses were silent by nature, so the snorts and low whinnies told her they were nervous.

"Probably because I'm lurking here in the dark, huh, guys?" Sam filled her voice with bravado.

Accustomed to the darkness now, her eyes finally made out shifting shadows of horses looking over the interior stall doors.

She was about to go striding in when a floorboard creaked.

No kidding? Sam chided herself. With a few tons of horses standing on it, a floor might creak?

Do it, Sam told herself. *Count down the stall doors to the fifth on the right. Touch her muzzle to make sure she's still there. After that, you can stop acting crazy and go home.*

Sam stepped inside.

If she were home, there'd be a flashlight on a shelf just inside the door. There'd be a lantern in the tack room.

Sam took a long step and trailed the fingers of her right hand against the first stall door. She heard the rustle of a horse moving in its bedding.

She took another step, counting off the second stall door as hooves thudded, startling back when the horse realized he didn't know her.

"It's okay, baby," she crooned.

At stall three, relief flowed through her. The welcome scent of a horse standing very close was followed by the velvet brush of its nose, extended in greeting. A frightened horse wouldn't be checking her out like that.

Something scuffed behind her. A shoe?

Sam looked over her shoulder. Though her brain insisted there had been movement, her eyes saw nothing.

She passed stall four.

When she reached five, there was a snort of recognition. Sweet alfalfa breath tickled her neck.

"Hi girl," Sam said, and her hand found the mare's cheek, sleek and smooth. "Were you patiently waiting for me to get down here and visit?"

Then everything happened at once. The mare's head jerked. She squealed in alarm. Outside the barn, Jed Kenworthy's irritated voice called, "Samantha!"

And a hand slammed between Sam's shoulder blades, driving her down the aisle.

"Hey!" she yelled, trying to dig in her heels.

But a second push propelled her a few steps before she stumbled through the feed room's open door.

She had to turn around. She had to get a look at him.

She had just enough breath to make a threatening sound as she wheeled toward the open feed room door, widening her eyes and filling them with nothing but shades of black.

A man's voice, but not a voice either, an almost apologetic mutter in his throat, made Sam hesitate. Should she jump at him? Try to tackle him down, since she'd just heard Jed Kenworthy who would surely back her up?

The flurry of thought only took a second, but it was long enough for the door to slam in her face.

She staggered backward until her spine slammed against the far wall. For a second, all was quiet and she was surrounded by the comforting smells of hay and grain.

But she had to get out of here. What was he doing? What was he keeping her from seeing? Did he mean to hurt the horses?

Sam pushed off from the wall, hard, and collided with the door. It budged just an inch before she heard something heavy scooting across the barn floor.

He was blocking her inside!

She felt dizzy and a little crazy. She thought of mustangs slamming themselves against wooden fence rails as she raced back to the wall again, gave herself a running start, and rammed into the door; but the stranger was stronger and he pushed back.

Sam cried out in surprise. She pounded, felt a sliver jab into the side of her fist, and yelled, "Let me out of here!"

She shoved with her shoulder, then listened.

The panting must have been hers, she realized, because the footsteps were running away.

He was gone.

She had to go out there, and yet something besides the weight against the door kept Sam trapped inside the feed room.

Four words flashed in her mind. She imagined they were scrawled in jagged scarlet letters across the black air in front of her.

Curiosity killed the cat.

Chapter Twelve ❧

$\mathcal{T}$he fear that had grabbed Sam by the throat loosened its grip.

It had to be Slocum who'd shoved her in here, didn't it?

But the next voice she heard wasn't Linc Slocum's.

"I'll be—" Jed Kenworthy's exasperated mutter told Sam that he was pretty angry. "What do they think? A man can see in the dark like a danged cat?"

Sam heard Jed slapping at the wall, searching for a light switch; then he bellowed, "You in here, Samantha?"

"Yes!" she shouted. "I'm trying to get out."

"Out of—?"

"I'm in the feed room, but something's pushed against it."

Sam tried shoving again. With a scraping sound, whatever it was budged just a little.

"Got it," Jed said with a grunt, and Sam realized he was helping from the other side. "How'd you get stuck in here?"

"In the dark, someone—I don't know who—but he pushed me in and I couldn't get out."

"Jen told me there'd been a boy hangin' around," Jed said in a joking tone. "That's why I came after you when the minutes kept tickin' off."

"I couldn't get out," she said again. "I kept trying and trying—"

"Samantha." Jed's tone was sympathetic, but he clearly thought it was time for her to settle down. "It only coulda lasted a minute."

Impossible, Sam thought.

"Well, I'm going to find whoever it was," she said, but she hadn't taken a step when a flashlight beam bisected the aisle.

Sam caught her breath, then recognized the security guard she'd seen outside talking to Linc. What a big help he'd been!

"Everything okay in here?" he shouted.

"Fine, just dumb kids and their pranks," Jed said.

A prank? Sam was about to ask Jed how he'd like to be stalked in the darkness, then shoved into a feed room. But of course she didn't.

Maybe she was being a little dramatic, but she hated the fact that no one cared enough to go after the guy.

Not that they could catch him now.

When the mare nuzzled her, Sam's hands loosened from fists she hadn't even known she'd made.

The security guard stood there looking awkward and useless as Jed lifted a stepladder off a wall hook, set it up beneath an overhead light, and stood on it.

"Someone was in here when I came in," Sam said, though neither man seemed too interested. "I don't know if he stole something or if he—"

Brightness filled the stable and Jed squinted as he finished screwing in a lightbulb and climbed down.

"Just got loosened with all the activity, I bet. Okay then," the guard said, heading for the door. "I'll let Mr. Ryden know everything's okay."

"Someone unscrewed that lightbulb. It didn't come loose on its own," Sam grumbled. "And it didn't feel like a prank."

"Don't blame you for feelin' that way," Jed said. "But I'll tell you, there's nothing on the face of God's green earth that's dumber than a teenage boy tryin' to get a girl's attention."

Jed was wrong.

Guys laughed when they were teasing, and they pulled pranks in groups.

Someone had shoved her into the feed room to get her out of the way, not to play a trick on her.

Frustrated by his response, Sam almost told Jed what she thought. But maybe he *did* believe her, because Jed was striding down the aisle, checking inside each stall.

"Horses look okay," Jed said. "This showy one's a little jumpy."

The chocolate mare rolled her eyes and backed away as Jed came near for a second look. She looked past him, head swinging toward the feed room, then back to the door that stood open to the night. She sniffed loudly and sweat darkened her neck.

"Let's take her with us," Sam blurted. "I just know that guy was trying to steal her."

"Not going to happen," Jed said. "Gettin' stolen, I mean. That fella"—Jed jerked his thumb toward the spot where the security guard had stood—"is gonna have his eyes open, now. Besides, Hal don't allow threats to his rodeo stock."

"She—the mare—isn't his, exactly. She just followed us in from the mountains when we were at the end of the drive."

"That so?" Jed's response wasn't really a question. "Tell me then, how Sheriff Ballard would see it any different if *we* took this here horse and loaded her up and hauled her off, compared to this fella that pushed you in with the oats?"

Jed's good sense and the long day's work settled like a concrete collar around Sam's neck. She gave in and led the way out of the barn.

She'd talk to Dad about this in the morning.

In Sam's dream the Phantom followed her.

With slow, light steps, the stallion and the girl crossed a bridge of magenta and lavender lights set on strands that were as thin as spiderwebs. Swaying above a black and immeasurable ravine, the delicate bridge supported them because together, their magic was strong.

Halfway across the span, Sam raised a flute to her lips. Enchanted notes floated up, iridescent as bubbles, and the Phantom playfully snapped them to tinier bubbles that drifted to his mane and clung to it like jewels. Prancing a unicorn dance, the stallion's moon-glow hide shone with dapples like ripples spreading on a silver pond.

Ace—mystical and wild, with crow feathers plaited into his mane—joined them as they stepped off the bridge of lights. Shoulder to shoulder, the threesome, with Sam in the middle, followed a tiny trickle of river through a concrete cavern with high sides. Confined, the river could never overflow into the city beyond.

The dream Phantom whinnied a worried call. Sam saw herself leading the horses on, as if she didn't know she led them into danger. But she knew.

When a cell door slammed behind them, Sam slipped through the bars like smoke, leaving the horses rearing inside, but her fists were the ones pounding to be free and her voice was the one screaming, "Let me out!"

Sam sat up with staring eyes. She had to go to the river. Now. She knew the Phantom was waiting for her in the moonlight. She knew—

It was morning.

She was home in her own bed at River Bend Ranch.

So why was she panting? Why did she feel so certain the Phantom was near?

Sunlight crept between her curtains, illuminating her patchwork quilt. Her open bedroom window let the smell of wild sweet peas float in, but she sure didn't hear the Phantom splashing in the river. The only sound was much nearer.

Cougar gave a disgruntled yowl because Sam had risen up and displaced him from his sleeping spot on her chest. He glared at her with yellow eyes before leaping off the bed.

As Sam watched her cat huff away, her breathing returned to normal.

The dream didn't mean anything.

Outside, Blaze the Border collie was barking. Maybe some sound from the ranch yard had found its way into her dream.

Someone was on the front porch, stamping dirt from their boots before coming into the kitchen.

Sam swung her legs out of bed. She grabbed a handful of nightgown and held it up so she didn't trip on her dash to her doorway. She listened down the stairs.

She heard Dad and Dallas, the ranch foreman, talking in the kitchen, but mixed in with their voices was a patting sound, like men pounding each other on the back in greeting. And there was a third voice she didn't quite recognize.

"Hal, let me get you some coffee, and I remember you always liked my pancakes." Gram's voice cut across the others. "With a little extra sugar sprinkled on top, am I right?"

Hal Ryden was in their kitchen!

Dad's boyhood friend had come to breakfast and she was missing it, Sam thought as she snatched up her jeans from her bedroom floor, then rummaged in a drawer for a fresh T-shirt.

Had he heard what had happened to her last night? Was he worried over the chocolate mare? Or had he just driven out to the ranch to say hi to his old rodeo pal?

She heard a door close and really hoped nothing interesting had ended before she'd even gotten out of bed. Why hadn't someone wakened her?

Barefoot, Sam ran down the stairs with Cougar beside her.

"This isn't a race," she told him, but Cougar didn't listen.

She grabbed the banister to keep from tripping as the tiger-striped cat cut her off, leaped the last three stairs, and careened into the kitchen ahead of her.

Hal Ryden sat at their kitchen table with a plateful of pancakes. He gave her an apologetic smile as she came in.

Sam was wondering why, but then she noticed Gram's and Dad's eyes fixed on her with concerned, accusing stares.

"What?" Sam asked.

"Samantha," Gram said, "why didn't you tell us you were locked into a stall—"

"Feed room," Sam corrected.

"—when you got home last night?"

"Because it was so late and everyone was asleep." Sam paused and glanced at Dad. "I figured—" she began, then stopped.

She couldn't explain how the notes Gram had left on the kitchen table—all with vague messages from Amelia's grandmother—had combined with the guilt she'd felt seeing Dad's broken-down truck.

"I figured. . ." She tried again, knowing the offer for Ace would help pay for a new truck.

Dad's brown eyes watched her over the rim of his coffee mug. If she mentioned the truck, would Dad be embarrassed in front of Hal Ryden?

"You figured what, Samantha?" Gram's voice urged Sam to go on.

Sam shrugged and finished, "That when I saw the truck sitting out there—"

"Dead as a doornail," Dad said in a smiling aside to Hal. "And a down payment on the one I want to replace it with is three thousand dollars, so I guess I'll see if I can resurrect the old darlin' one more time."

"—that there was enough going on without me waking everyone up," Sam said, managing to finish her sentence.

The previous night, she'd led Ace across the bridge. The truck hadn't been pushed very far from where it had broken down in the middle of the bridge, and because Jed's cattle trailer was extra wide, it wouldn't fit.

Sam hadn't minded the late-night walk with her horse.

The La Charla River had prattled beneath them. Cool drifts of air wafted up from its surface. If Ace hadn't been pulling so hard on his lead rope, Sam would have taken him wading.

But Ace had lifted his knees in eagerness. Once they reached the silent ranch yard, his ears swiveled. Did he hear a field mouse running for its burrow as a wide-winged owl cruised overhead? Were his mustang ears sensitive enough to recognize the brush of Tempest's black muzzle, nudging her mother for a midnight snack, all the way from the barn?

As she'd slid back the bolt on the gate, Strawberry had crowded forward, reminding Sam which horse ruled the ten-acre pasture. Ace had bobbed his head and brushed past the roan. Sam had left him grunting and rolling as if the grass of home could remove the stench of the city from his coat.

Is that what her dream had been about? Selling Ace and banishing him to the city while she stayed on the ranch? But the nightmare hadn't just made her feel guilty. Panic from the moments she'd been locked in the feed room had rushed back, along with the eerie feeling that it was no coincidence that the down payment on the truck Dad wanted was exactly the same amount that Amelia's grandmother had offered for Ace.

Suddenly Sam realized everyone's watchfulness had changed from impatience to concern.

Feeling sheepish, Sam said, "It was no big deal. Last night I was scared, but now I'm not."

In the daylight, at home, she was pretty sure she'd been worried over nothing.

"I was going to tell you first thing this morning," she insisted. She glanced at Gram, whose spatula was poised over a griddle filled with pancakes. "Shouldn't I wait for Brynna to come down?"

Her stepmother had been rising a little later on weekends since she'd become pregnant. Sam knew, though, that Brynna would not only be interested, but helpful, as well.

"She's down and already out on a ride," Dad said, and when Gram shook her head in disapproval, he added, "She a fine rider and she's on Strawberry."

"You can tell us now, Samantha," Gram said, "and we'll fill her in when she gets back."

So Sam did, recounting all that had happened from the moment she and Jen had spotted the boy petting the chocolate mare and calling her his lass, to the minute Jed had hustled Sam into the crowded truck cab for the ride home.

"So it's no big deal, I guess," Sam said, finishing her story. "Jen's dad said someone was just playing a joke on me."

Hal met Dad's eyes across the table. When neither of them spoke, Sam glanced at Gram, surprised that Gram was looking at her, and not at the food cooking on the stove.

When Gram caught Sam's gaze, she looked down, tsked her tongue, and scooted the spatula under a smoking pancake.

"Burned to a crisp," Gram muttered as she flipped it toward a plate.

"You mighta interrupted a robbery," Hal said. "After the fairground security guard came and told me about the light being out and you being pushed into the feed room—well, it just sounded all wrong."

Sam couldn't help smiling. She knew Hal Ryden was like Dad and Jake. If something didn't seem right, they'd investigate.

"I got suspicious and went out to check. No offense to that security guard, you understand, but I asked some of my own people to help me take a look around, and it was a good thing we did.

"We found a little cotton rope that no one recognized. Now that wouldn't have looked like evidence to the sheriff, but moving around the way we do, from rodeo to rodeo, we know every piece of our gear and keep track of it.

"Not only wasn't the rope ours; it was tied into a war bridle."

"I don't know what that is," Sam said, although she didn't like the sound of it.

"Sometimes you see them on Indian ponies in the old movies," Hal said. "Just like a hand-tied halter, only a loop's tied around the horse's lower jaw."

"That, plus the horse thief we had around here," Dad said, "made us think you mighta walked in on something."

The knot of muscle that bulged at Dad's jaw told her he was angry, and she was pretty sure his fury was aimed at her.

"I'm sorry it never crossed my mind that there would be horse theft problems here," Hal said. "This is one of the smaller towns we pass through."

"Not your fault," Dad said. "That's the heck of it. There's no one to blame."

Except Linc Slocum, Sam thought, but she only asked, "Which horse do you think they were after?"

"Hard to say," Hal told her. "But I have an idea it wasn't one of my blacks—though they're all valuable—probably not Criollo or Cloudburst, my roping horses, or your friend's palomino, though she's an outstanding-looking animal."

"Silk Stockings," Dad told him. "A little bit loco, but she's one of the Kenworthy palominos."

"But Silly wasn't in the barn when I came back," Sam put in.

"But you *rode* out," Hal said. "I saw you. And I knew you were goin' home. Anyone else would have guessed you were just going out for a moonlight ride. Our thief mighta been waiting for you to come back."

Sam shivered. It was beyond creepy to think someone had been in the barn, watching and waiting while they'd been saddling up and chattering about Ace's misbehavior. But Hal had said he was pretty sure the thief *wasn't* after the horses he'd mentioned.

"I think the thief wanted the mare that followed us down from the mountains," Hal said. "That war bridle was inside her stall."

"I knew it!" Sam shouted. Gram frowned at the threads of maple syrup that dripped as Sam gestured with her fork. She lay the fork back on her plate and said, more quietly, "I knew it, and you want to know who planned it?"

Sam felt like a movie detective, who calmly solved the mystery after everyone else had been running around in confusion.

"Of course we do, dear," Gram said. "But eat breakfast while you talk."

Just to satisfy Gram, Sam took a bite, then said, "Linc was mean to me yesterday."

"I heard what he said." In a disapproving tone, Hal told Dad and Gram about the "welcome as a rattlesnake" remark he'd overheard.

"That man can make being a good neighbor pretty difficult," Gram said, "but—"

"No, Gram, that was just the beginning," Sam rushed on. "He also told me that curiosity killed the cat."

"Honey, I believe you," Dad assured her. "But why did he say that?"

"He wants to be part of the rodeo association," Sam explained. "And he thinks what I know about him could ruin his reputation."

Dad gave a short, bitter laugh.

"Now, Wyatt," Gram cautioned.

"Didn't say a word. Though if I had, I'd say Linc doesn't need help makin' himself look bad."

"Still," Hal began, looking dubious. "It's a big leap from mean talk to horse theft. You think the sheriff will go along with your finger pointing?"

Sam mulled that over for a second. Sheriff Ballard insisted on evidence. He'd lectured her about that before.

She turned her argument toward Dad.

"I know this seems far-fetched, but remember Karl Mannix?" Sam asked.

"He's a horse thief, and even though he's not a very good one, he worked for Linc and he got away. Plus, he knows how Linc loves unusual livestock."

"I'm not following you," Hal said, and he looked even more skeptical when Dad explained that Karl Mannix had stolen horses from the Gold Dust Ranch. "So, because he's done it before and is kinda inept at handling horses, you think it's him. I get that part. But surely Slocum's not gonna buy a horse from a man who stole from him."

"There's a chance that Linc didn't discourage him from stealing the colt," Dad said.

"A chance?" Gram snapped, adding two more pancakes to Sam's stack. "Why, it's plain as red paint that Linc thought his son was too softhearted when it came to that half-breed colt." Then, looking surprised by her own outburst, Gram said, "Don't listen to a word I say, Samantha. I'm just a cranky old woman."

Sam laughed. Gram meant what she'd said.

"Hal, if the man sees something he wants, he goes

after it," Dad admitted. "Brynna's been trying to catch him tracking a certain range stallion. And that's a federal crime."

The Phantom, Sam thought. The stallion still wore scars inflicted by Linc's attempt to capture him.

"What we're saying," Gram added, quietly, "is we wouldn't put it past him."

"And he collects weird livestock," Sam told Hal.

"You keep sayin' that. What qualifies this mare as weird livestock?" Dad asked.

"Unusual." Sam corrected herself, picturing the white-gold mane that fell to the mare's smooth, dark shoulders. "You should see her."

She was about to describe the mare's unusual coloring when the phone began ringing. Sam hoped everyone ignored it. She didn't want to talk with Amelia's grandmother and she had the queasy feeling that that was who was calling so early.

"No sooner said than done. C'mon out, Wyatt, Grace," Hal was saying, pushing back from the table, then carrying his plate toward the sink while Gram was still deciding whether to do it for him or answer the phone.

C'mon out? Sam thought. Could she blame her confusion on trying to listen to Gram's phone conversation?

"Are we driving back to the fairgrounds?" Sam asked.

"I guess that's what you get for sleepin' late," Hal teased.

"What did I miss?" Sam asked.

"I talked this whole situation over with the sheriff, and while he didn't think there was reason enough to stake out the rodeo with a deputy, he agreed that the mare might be safer here at River Bend Ranch."

Chapter Thirteen ❧

Sam considered the phone Gram extended as if she were offering a poisonous snake.

"Samantha," Gram said reproachfully, "it's Lynn Cooper, the reporter."

"Oh," Sam said, relieved, and hurried to answer.

"Hi, there," Lynn said. "I hear you had a little excitement last night."

"Yeah," Sam said. "How did you know?"

"I'll explain later," Lynn said. "Just now, I'd like to talk to your dad and see if he'll allow you to come back to the rodeo to help me out with this horse story."

Sam's eyes wandered to Dad. "I can't think of any reason he'd care," she said. Then she noticed Dad's eyebrows arching in question. "But I'll let you talk to him."

As usual, when Dad "talked" on the telephone, he said almost nothing, but Sam could tell he wasn't entirely happy with what Lynn was saying.

"Nope, I don't think that will work," he said, finally.

"What?" Sam yelped.

Dad gave her a look that said he wouldn't welcome another outburst and listened some more.

"Not until they get the security situation nailed down," he said.

"Oh my gosh," Sam muttered as she paced in frustration. "I'm fourteen years old."

It was weird, but she hadn't known how much she wanted to help Lynn with the story until Dad refused to let her do it.

She was staring at Dad, watching his face for a sign that he was changing his mind, when she noticed Hal slipping on the black cowboy hat he'd hung on the rack by the front door.

"Samantha, honey, take it from an old rodeo rider," Hal said, nodding at Dad. "Don't mess with the bull 'less you're willin' to deal with them horns."

Then, before she'd quite figured that out, he made a polite nod and said, "Ladies, I've got a mare to unload. I'll see you outside."

In the end, Dad agreed Sam could help on the

story from home and she could talk with Lynn. That was all.

Gram had left the kitchen and followed Hal when Dad covered the mouthpiece and told her, "We'll talk about your behavior later."

Then Dad handed her the phone. She held it as he put on his Stetson, gave her a frown over his shoulder, and left without a word.

There was no way she'd sell her horse to buy Dad a new truck. He could just walk.

Okay, I'm acting like a brat, Sam told herself. *He's just trying to keep me safe. As usual, it's totally unnecessary.*

But Lynn was waiting.

Sam took a deep breath and said, "Hi, again."

"First off, I don't blame him. If you were my daughter, I wouldn't want you locked in a stall."

"Feed room," Sam corrected.

"Really?" Lynn stretched the word out. "I heard a stall."

"I could have unbolted a stall, or climbed over," Sam explained, thinking it was weird that Gram had said the same thing. Is that what Hal had told her? Maybe the guard had got it wrong when he told Hal.

"Anyway, tell me your ideas for proceeding with the story," Lynn said, "and we'll work out what you can do from home."

"Wait, who told you about last night?"

"Linc Slocum."

"I knew it!" Sam crowed for the second time that morning. "That guy is out to get me."

Since Lynn already knew that Linc thought Sam was nosy, she explained the rest of her theory, just as she had to Hal, Dad, and Gram.

Lynn was quiet for a minute. Sam heard her take a sip of something before she answered. "What have you got for proof?" she asked finally.

"I told you—he thinks I'm ruining his reputation."

"And for that, he'd buy a stolen horse? Think a minute, Sam. It doesn't make sense."

"But if he told you about what happened to me, it means he knew."

"He's not alone. That rodeo's like a gossipy small town."

"Really?" Sam asked quietly. "So, what about— wait. Sheriff Ballard told me when you're looking for suspects in any crime, you search for motive and opportunity." Sam felt suddenly sure of herself. "Linc collects exotic livestock—there's the motive—and he was standing right outside the barn when the thief was inside. I'd call that opportunity."

"Let's try this, then," Lynn said. "You were around the barn all afternoon and had access to it and a stock trailer, all night. And you, unlike Linc Slocum, showed a whole lot of interest in that mare. For witnesses, there's Jen, the vet, Hal, and me."

"What are you saying?" Sam asked.

"Motive and opportunity," Lynn said. "You had

more of both than he did and it still means nothing."

"I thought you were looking for a hot news story," Sam grumbled.

"I am. We've opened the mystery of the mountain mare and I want a follow-up. Better than that, I want to discover her owner."

"Okay," Sam said. "But while we're investigating that, what if—"

"Forget about your feud with Linc Slocum and find some facts," Lynn said, laughing lightly. "Here's what you learn in journalism school, Sam: The public has a right to know the truth. If you don't have the truth, if you start showing news stories that attack someone's character just because you're pretty sure they did something wrong, you're committing libel and you can go to jail for it."

Sam blew out her cheeks. She hadn't thought investigative journalism would be so hard.

"That makes sense," she admitted finally. "But what if I *know* he's guilty?"

Lynn's tone was absolutely no-nonsense when she said, "Find evidence to back up what you're saying. Otherwise, forget it."

Sam couldn't help looking toward the river when she stepped onto the front porch. The Phantom wouldn't be there in the daylight. And she couldn't see the wild side of the river from here.

Though the dream hadn't been real, her thoughts kept spinning around the Phantom.

"You have a beautiful spread, right here in the river's elbow, with the mountain range on the horizon," Hal Ryden said as he stared toward the Calico Mountains. "Growing up around here, I just took it for granted."

"Hal's family used to own the Crane Crossing Ranch," Gram told Sam.

"Crane Crossing? Like the mall?" Sam asked.

"That was it," Hal said with a melancholy grin. "You'd never think so to look at it now, but it was a beautiful ranch. Kinda ironic that they poured asphalt for the parking lots over the wetlands, then named the whole shebang after the birds that can't come there anymore." Hal scuffed a boot in the dirt and studied it as he said, "My old man just didn't have the backbone to stand up against the developers."

"Sometimes it takes more than backbone," Gram said.

As all three adults nodded, Sam knew they were talking about money again.

"Yeah, I heard old man Potter sold the Happy Heart Ranch and became a millionaire," Hal said. "Well, I'll tell you, I've been lucky that rodeo has worked out for me. I've got my place in Montana and I love it. It's like those wild horses we were talking about—even though we don't see 'em much, we like knowing they're there. That's how I feel about my ranch." Hal clapped Dad on the back. "And I'm real glad you all are makin' a go of it."

"It's not easy," Dad said. "Take a day like today, for instance. One problem just leads to another. Truck's dead, so I've got to ride horseback out to fix the irrigation system. While I'm doing that, horse could throw a shoe, and by the time I rode her home to fix it, she's pulled a muscle favoring that hoof, leading to a vet bill or at least a new tin of liniment."

Dad pretended he was joking, but Sam knew he wasn't when he went on, "Sometimes I wonder if folks aren't right, that we're hanging onto a way of life that's seen its day. Why run cattle on the open range, folks ask, when they can be kept in feedlots next to the factories and just be processed from birth to death?"

"I guess we know why," Gram said, sniffing as she crossed her arms. "Because when you cram all those creatures in together, they get sick and their meat gives you horrid diseases."

"Yeah, you're right," Dad said, then he turned back to Hal. "We're just hoping we can keep River Bend Ranch until the kids are grown."

The kids. Dad must have told Hal that Brynna was expecting a baby. It wasn't much of a secret anymore.

"'River Bend' is a terrible name for a mall anyway," Hal said, and though Dad and Gram chuckled, their laughter was grim. "Before you get to that point, Samantha here will go off to college and make you all rich."

Did photojournalists get rich? Sam hoped so, because she hated what she was hearing.

"Sam knows what's important, and it's not just money," Dad said confidently. "She loves this ranch and she does her part."

Not if my part is selling Ace! Sam bit her lip to hold back the words.

"She's a good girl," Gram seconded, patting Sam on the back. Then, changing the subject, she said, "Sam, before I forget, why is that lady from Albuquerque calling you every time I turn around?"

"It's Amelia's grandmother," Sam said. She swallowed, before going on. "She wants to talk to me about horses."

It was true enough, Sam thought.

Then, even though the mare picked her way around the ranch yard at the end of a leather lead, showing off her graceful gaits and beautiful coloring, Sam didn't watch her. Instead, Sam stared at the horses she'd seen a thousand times.

In the ten-acre pasture, Tank and Amigo grazed together. They might have been a display for what Quarter Horse conformation and muscles built by hard work should look like. Blood-bay Nike and Appaloosa Jeepers-Creepers looked tall and speedy, though they were just grazing beside Sweetheart, Gram's aged pinto. Ace, Popcorn, and Penny, all mustangs, were on alert, studying the chocolate mare. Even Penny's blindness couldn't keep wild instincts from telling her never to ignore something new.

When Blaze investigated the strange horse trailer and knocked against a bucket, the mustangs fled. Ace led their charge for the far end of the pasture.

That's how mustangs were, Sam thought. And maybe that alertness, that instinct to run from danger, wasn't such a good trait for a therapy horse.

Then again, she might just be telling herself that so she didn't lose Ace.

She stared out at the Calico Mountains, as Hal had. Up there somewhere was the Phantom's secret valley. The surrounding territory held Lost Canyon, Arroyo Azul, the Deerpath Ranch's mysterious hot springs, and Aspen Creek's trembling leaves.

I love this place, she thought. And what about Dad and Gram? If they had to leave the ranch and live in the city, they'd wither and become completely different people.

Dad and Gram didn't take a single day on the ranch for granted. Regardless of the weather, they greeted each morning as if they'd embrace it, filling their eyes with vaulting sky and sagebrush-covered ridges. Then they gave silent prayers of thanks for living the life they loved.

"Easiest way to figure out who she belongs to is to check her for a chip," Hal was saying when Sam refocused on the conversation around her. "I've already looked for brands and a lip tattoo."

A chip! Of course, lots of horses had microchips inserted in their necks. Each microchip was supposed to have an individual number on it that could be read instantly with a scanner. The vet had mentioned it, too.

"Where do we get a scanner?" Sam asked suddenly.

"There are all kinds of chips and all kinda scanners," Dad said.

"Yeah," Hal said slowly. "I keep hearing about a universal scanner, but I don't know if they make 'em yet. And those little chips can migrate from the neck to other places in the body, too, so we'd best think of someone who knows what he's doing."

"Sheriff Ballard?" Gram suggested.

Sam was already running toward the house when she heard Hal say that might be a good place to start.

Chapter Fourteen ❧

"**H**aven't had a call from anyone who recognized that horse on TV and it seems awful strange to me," Sheriff Ballard said. "Horses can travel some distance, but I figured her for a local mare, since she looked to be in fine shape—"

Sheriff Hector Ballard was one of Sam's favorite people. With his droopy mustache and brown hair that needed trimming, he looked just like the small-town sheriff he was, but he used every spare minute to improve his skills and every spare penny for high-tech equipment. Besides that, he was a horseman.

Sam wasn't a bit surprised he'd been thinking about the mare.

"—until I noticed she was a Rocky Mountain Horse."

"A what?" Sam asked.

"'Course, I haven't seen her in the flesh, but from the TV news, she looked to me like a Rocky Mountain Horse, just her coloring. You've seen her move around, Sam. Does she move like a gaited horse? Sort of an ambling way of going, but it looks real natural, not like she was schooled to it?"

"That's it exactly," Sam said.

The sheriff made a satisfied sound.

"Good chance, then, that she's a Rocky. Someone'll be missing her. Looking for a chip's a good start. You could check with the Department of Agriculture," the sheriff mused. "But it'd be quicker if I got in touch with Duke Fairchild."

"Duke?" Sam asked. She'd been expecting Sheriff Ballard to suggest someone in law enforcement.

"Duke's the most careful man I know for establishing ownership. He checks for hot brands, freeze brands, tattoos, chips, and any other thing. He's got a phobia about selling a stolen horse at his auction yards. Especially since that Baldy Harris from Dagdown Packing spends so much of his company's money there."

Sam grimaced. Baldy Harris bought horses for meat.

"I think that would be great," Sam said. "And since I'm practically grounded, I'll sit right here and wait for him."

"Grounded, huh?" the sheriff sounded more amused than sympathetic. "What'd you go and do now, Samantha?"

"It wasn't me," Sam started.

"Got it," the sheriff said. "Your dad's keeping you close to home after last night."

It made sense that rodeo security or Hal or someone had told Sheriff Ballard, but she was beginning to feel like the main dish at a buffet.

When she stayed quiet, he said, "Bet you got your own theory about who shoved you in there."

"I do," Sam said, but Lynn Cooper's reaction, on top of Gram and Dad's, made her keep her theory to herself.

"It involve anyone we know?" he asked.

It almost choked her not to shout, Linc Slocum! It's him! I know it is!

Sam just said, "Yes, but I'm working on finding *evidence* and *motive*."

She must have sounded sarcastic, because the sheriff laughed.

Sam could hear the smile in his voice as he said, "Can I count on you to let me know if anything turns up?"

"Of course," she said.

"And before I ask Duke Fairchild to have someone bring over a scanner, I want a promise you won't go charging off trying to fix things on your own."

Sheriff Ballard's tone turned stern.

"I won't," Sam said, and it was the truth.

Dad wasn't going to let her off the ranch, but that didn't mean she couldn't use the phone and Internet to help Lynn solve the mystery—she imagined dramatic music—of the mountain mare.

"I can see she's in good hands," Hal said after Sam had returned to the ranch yard and told him, Dad, and Gram what the sheriff had said.

"My lands, Samantha," Gram said, wide-eyed. "That was quick."

Sam was about to tell Gram that Lynn had said, that Sam had "a nose for news," and it had led her directly to a good source. But she didn't get a chance to brag.

"Heck Ballard's a good sheriff," Dad said, but he must have seen Sam's smile fade, because he squeezed the back of her neck. "You want to take care of that horse and tell Brynna—if she ever gets home—the whole story? I don't have the patience, but I do have some danged irrigation pipes to fix."

"Sure, Dad," Sam said.

All buckaroos hated jobs they couldn't do from the back of a horse, and for her father, equipment malfunctions were the worst.

Hal had tied the mare to the hitching rail near the round pen. As he drove away, Gram and Sam went to pamper the horse.

"Hey, pretty girl," Sam said to the mare. "We're

going to find your family right away."

"She's very gentle and sweet, isn't she?" Gram said as the mare rested her chin on Sam's shoulder. "I'd call that almost a hug."

Sam stood very still, letting the mare sniff and investigate her hair.

"I'll go look for some carrots," Gram said. "That'll pass the time 'til that scanner gets here. I do hope it's nothing that will hurt her."

Duke Fairchild arrived as the mare took a second carrot from Gram then bobbed her head in crunching delight.

"Good morning, Grace," Duke Fairchild greeted Gram. "And Sam, good to see you, too. Sorry we didn't get to talk on that rodeo cattle drive. Kind of fun, wasn't it?"

Duke Fairchild's blue eyes seemed brighter because of his silver hair, and though no one would mistake him for a cowboy, his Western-styled shirt and polished boots suited him.

"Thanks so much for coming out," Gram said.

"My pleasure," he said. "I'm excited about using this new gadget of mine. It's a universal chip reader. Supposed to pick up any brand of microchip."

Duke stood near the mare, letting her get used to him, before he slid his hand under her mane.

"Are you feeling for the chip?" Sam asked.

"No, it's tiny, about the size of a grain of rice,

and it's injected someplace between her poll and withers, under this ligament."

The mare accepted Duke's hands as easily as she had Sam and Gram's, and when he took out the scanner, she just sniffed it.

"Will it hurt her?" Gram asked.

"Naw, it's just like a store's bar scanner, least that's what I've been told, and if it's anything like the older ones I've used, she'll only react to the beeping that starts up when I find the chip."

"How can you be sure it's still there?" Gram asked.

"Once chips are in, they're there for life," Duke said, as he hovered the scanner over the mare's neck. "They can migrate, but they don't usually go very far."

"And when it beeps, what happens next?" Sam asked.

"Depends on the registry, but most folks these days are registered so that we'll get a read out of the owner's name and phone number right here," Duke said, tapping a little window on the scanner, "on the display."

"That sounds like magic," Gram said, "when I think back on lost horses we've come across after floods and fires."

"We'll have you back in your stall before you know it," Sam told the mare. "I wish Brynna were here."

"She'd get a kick out of it, all right," Gram said.

"This all assumes the mare has a chip," Duke cautioned. "I'm not picking anything up just yet."

"I'll go get you a cup of coffee," Gram offered, but just then Duke gave an exclamation.

"Hey! We got it!"

Even then, the mare didn't startle. Sam thought she regarded the excited humans with amused patience.

"Let me see!" Gram said, crowding past Sam. "Oh, let me get a pencil so we can write it down."

Gram hustled into the house and back while Duke showed Sam the electronic display. "Frank McKenzie is her owner, and here's his phone number. This is a great little toy," Duke muttered. "And I'll put it to good use."

"I'll call him!" Sam said. "Can I?"

"Go ahead, dear," Gram said. "After all, this was your idea."

Excitement over her good deed pushed Sam's worries aside. She dialed the unfamiliar area code and waited as the phone rang.

"McKenzie Farms," said a businesslike male voice. "This is Jack."

"We found your horse!" Sam blurted.

She waited for the voice to burst into celebration.

"What horse would that be? And who's calling?"

It must be a huge farm if they didn't know they'd lost a horse like that beautiful mare, Sam thought.

Sam heard the kitchen door open, but she ignored it. Not only did she feel let down, but she wished someone who appreciated the horse had answered the phone.

"My name is Samantha Forster and I'm calling from River Bend Ranch in northern Nevada. We just scanned a mare, probably a Rocky Mountain Horse, and the microchip came up with your name and number."

In the moment of silence that followed, Sam could hear stable sounds from somewhere far away. Water whooshed into a metal bucket. A horse neighed.

"This is Frank McKenzie, isn't it?" Sam asked. Could the microchip have given the scanner the wrong phone number?

"Ms. Forster," the voice said finally, "I'm Mr. McKenzie's stable manager, and I do thank you for calling, but this must be a horse we sold after we had it chipped. We're not missing any horses."

"I could describe her for you," Sam offered.

"Everything's computerized here at McKenzie Farms, Ms. Forster. You'd be wasting your time. I can tell you without a doubt that the horse doesn't belong here. Good luck."

"No, wait. Here's a number. That might help." She read it quickly, not giving him a chance to refuse.

He didn't.

"Got it," he said, "and I'm transferring you to someone who can look that up." Annoyed, but hoping the mystery was about to be solved, Sam waited. She heard a click and the rapid tapping of computer keys.

"Hello?" Sam asked.

"I ran an inquiry on that number," said a female voice that sounded busy, but a little friendlier. "It refers to McKenzie's Blackstrap Molasses, a twelve-year-old broodmare, chocolate and white, put down last week because of retinal detachment."

"Put down," Sam repeated. "Destroyed, you mean?"

"Well, yes."

"But—" Sam stared at the kitchen wall as if she could see through it to the gentle mare tied outside.

"I'll call our chip supplier and remind them to update their records. Or maybe they've already reassigned the number. Who knows? Anyway, thanks for the heads up."

Sam was still listening to the dial tone when she looked over to see Brynna standing in the kitchen, face flushed with exertion.

"Hi," Sam said. She crossed her arms, trying to figure out where to begin her explanation. First, she'd have to unravel what had just happened.

Instead of dancing around in celebration because she'd found the mare's grieving owner, she'd just heard the horse was dead. Except she obviously wasn't.

Brynna was studying the piece of paper bearing the useless phone number as if it were written in code. Maybe she was exhausted from her ride. She did smell pretty horsy, and Strawberry could be a handful.

"Do you want some orange juice?" Sam asked. "Or ice water?"

Was Brynna hypnotized? She shook her head slowly and tapped the piece of paper with her index finger.

"No," Brynna said. She pushed loosened strands of red hair back toward a disheveled braid as she met Sam's eyes. "What I want is for you to make that same phone call to a different number and let me know what you hear."

Chapter Fifteen ∾

$\mathcal{B}$rynna grabbed the telephone book, flipped through the flimsy pages, then turned it toward Sam.

"Dial that, and ask for room 224."

"I'm calling the hospital?" Sam asked. Maybe Brynna really was losing it.

"You're calling Diana McKenzie."

Sam sucked in a deep breath.

Frank McKenzie owned the chocolate mare.

Diana McKenzie was the girl who'd been hurt in the car accident with the empty horse trailer.

Except maybe the trailer hadn't been empty. Why had Diana insisted it was? Why wouldn't she beg the sheriff to go after her escaped horse? And why did McKenzie Farms think the mare was dead?

"Just dial," Brynna said, fanning herself with her hand, and Sam did.

The phone rang seven times. Sam was about to hang up when the receiver sounded as if it were being juggled up to someone's ear.

"Hello?"

"Diana? This is Sam Forster—"

"Miss McKenzie's just checking out. I'm the nurse's aide."

"Could you please catch her for me?" Sam asked. "It's really important."

"She's halfway down the hall—"

Hurry up and think, Sam told her brain.

"I, uh, found something she lost in the accident." Sam grimaced at how lame she sounded, but it was all she could come up with, and she thought it was true.

Judging by Brynna's thumbs-up, it was okay.

"I'll get her," said the nurse's aide.

"Hello?"

When she heard Diana McKenzie's concerned voice, Sam pictured the dark-haired girl with hazel eyes who'd looked so weak sitting in the rodeo first aid center.

"Hi Diana, this is Samantha Forster, I met you—"

"I remember," Diana said cautiously. "You were with that reporter and . . ." She paused. "And your mother stayed with me while they admitted me to the hospital."

"I'm calling because we found your horse!" Sam

tried to sound excited, just as she had before. "We just scanned a mare, probably a Rocky Mountain Horse, and the microchip came up with your name and number."

Just as before, when she'd called McKenzie Farms, there was silence. Then Sam heard whispers and a jumbling sound as the telephone receiver changed hands. This time it was broken by a male voice.

"Can you give me directions to your ranch? We need to see the horse."

"Uh, sure," Sam said. She'd expected a longer conversation leading up to this point. "Just a second."

Sam knew Brynna would do a better job of giving lefts and rights out of Darton to the freeway, so she handed her the phone and sat listening until Brynna hung up.

"Now I'll take that juice," Brynna said, leaning back in her chair at the kitchen table.

"What's going on?" Sam asked as she poured juice for them both.

"I'm not exactly sure, but I think it's a good thing the boyfriend—Diana said his name was Kevin, right?"

Sam nodded.

"I think Kevin's involved, too."

"In what, though?"

"My guess is that Diana had the mare in the trailer during the accident, and then the horse either got loose or Diana turned her loose.

"*Why* is the hard part," Brynna said before Sam could ask.

"Should we call the sheriff?" Sam asked instead.

"I think we can wait on that, and on telling your dad," Brynna said with a conspiratorial wink. "Because I think Kevin's the one who locked you in the feed room."

"Kevin," Sam said blankly, before another thought shoved that one aside. "How did you know about me being locked in the feed room?"

"I rode into Alkali for one of Clara's sweet rolls," Brynna whispered, glancing toward the ranch yard. "Don't tell your gram."

"I won't, but—"

"You were the talk of the diner," Brynna told her.

Her stepmother was watching to make sure she took the information with good humor, so Sam just smiled instead of groaning or letting her head sag into her hands in humiliation.

"The timing's right," Brynna said. "Kevin arrived as Diana was being admitted to the hospital. When we'd gotten her settled in her room, he clicked on the television just as Lynn's story about the mystery mare came on the six o'clock news."

Sam thought back to last night. At six o'clock, she and Jen would have been window-shopping or buying corn dogs and lemonade.

"We all sat there watching," Brynna recalled. "But then, come to think of it . . . Yeah," Brynna said, nodding. "It was just after she saw the mare do that bowing trick that Diana was sick again. She went all pale and wobbly, but when I offered to call a nurse, she just said she wanted to rest." Brynna shrugged. "And to tell you the truth, I was feeling a little tired myself, so I left, but now I'm remembering the kind of . . . ," Brynna paused, searching for a word, "*intense* looks she was flashing Kevin."

Sam and Brynna were still talking, working through "what ifs," an hour later, when Blaze began barking.

"It could be them," Sam said.

She looked out the front window in time to see Blaze rush toward the bridge as he increased the volume of his barking.

"It is," Brynna said as a yellow Scout pulling a horse trailer edged past Dad's dead truck and into the ranch yard.

Gram stood up from pulling weeds in her garden, and for the first time Sam saw the chocolate mare become agitated.

Diana climbed carefully from the passenger's side of the yellow vehicle. She scanned the ranch buildings. Then she spotted the horse. She took one cautious step, as if she were balancing her head on her shoulders.

She must still hurt, Sam thought, but when the mare released a longing neigh, Diana went running.

The mare pulled as far from the hitching rail as

her rope would allow. She stretched her nose toward the girl, closing the distance between them every inch she could until Diana wrapped her arms around the mare's neck.

"Careful, Di," said the guy striding from the truck.

Instantly, Sam recognized him. He was the one who'd been crooning to the mare yesterday, calling her his lass.

McKenzie's Blackstrap Molasses, Sam thought, suddenly.

Molasses. Her stable name could be Lass.

The mare's excited, bobbing head bumped and loosened a bandage from over Diana's ear. The girl bent and retrieved it, then shoved it into her pocket as the mare nibbled her hair.

"I'm sorry," Diana said to the horse.

Or was it to them? Sam wondered, as she and Brynna joined Gram.

Kevin stood in front of Sam. He blushed and swallowed so hard, she heard it.

"And I'm really sorry about last night. I'd come to get Lass and I didn't exactly know what I was doing. I mean, Lass does tricks and she was used to that war bridle, but I wasn't. When you came back, I didn't expect you and I kind of panicked. I hope you're okay."

"I am," Sam said. "My arms are sore, though."

"No kidding," he said with a short laugh. "You hit that door like a linebacker."

Sam couldn't help smiling. It was just the sort of compliment Jake would give.

"We need to talk," Brynna interrupted.

It was her official voice, and no one mistook it for friendly. Kevin's smile melted and Diana's arms dropped from her horse's neck.

"Let's do it inside," Gram said, and Sam noticed she didn't mention anything about food.

"It's all my fault," Diana said once they were seated around the kitchen table. "And I don't blame you if you want to press charges. I know I broke some laws, but more than that, I—" Diana's voice cracked and she began to cry. "Deserted my horse. She almost died because of me."

Sam remembered her dream. Ace and the Phantom had radiated feelings of betrayal at her. Sam wet her lips, ready to sympathize with Diana, when Brynna touched Sam's arm and shook her head.

"I went away to school and just forgot about her," Diana said. "Not really. I could never forget Lass, but I don't think I've ridden her since my senior year in high school. And Dad started using her as a brood-mare, which is fine, but I went home and I heard that they were going to have her destroyed because of some hereditary eye problem."

Brynna stirred beside her and Sam knew this time it was her stepmother who wanted to interrupt. Brynna's blind mare meant the world to her, and she'd have a lot to say about someone destroying a horse because of eye problems.

"But here's the thing," Kevin cut in. "The retinal detachment problem that Jack was blabbing about doesn't cause blindness. I've done some research and it *is* more common in Rocky Mountain Horses, Morgans, and some miniature horses, but it might not even be hereditary."

"So why was he putting her down?" Gram asked.

"He called her a *hay burner*," Diana sneered. "He actually said that to my face. That's when I just snapped. Jack, our stable manager, is really good at what he does and he's made my dad lots of money, but he just said it was time to take her out of the breeding program." Diana looked at each of them. "I understand that, but why kill her?"

Just like Linc Slocum, Sam thought. He'd wanted to "cull" Shy Boots, Ryan's colt, because he couldn't be registered.

Sam drew a breath then. The more Diana talked, the less it looked like Slocum was involved. How could she have been wrong?

"So you were taking her away," Sam said. Diana nodded. "But did you turn her loose? You know she was up in the mountains, with a wild stallion. She could have been hurt."

"I know. Abandoning her while I was at school was the first stupid thing I did, but letting her make her own choice was the second," Diana said, shaking her head. "I was crying, and I ran off the road, and the trailer—" Diana covered her ears as if she still heard the mare's distressed neighs. "When I let her out, she bolted. And, I don't know, I guess I thought she'd be happier that way, out in the wild. . . ."

As Diana's voice trailed off, Brynna sat up straighter and cleared her throat.

"It was not only a silly choice, it was an illegal one," Brynna said.

Gram's glance said she thought Brynna was being harsh, but Sam understood.

"It's like people who dump unwanted dogs and think they'll fend for themselves," Brynna went on. "It doesn't work. Domestic animals, especially older ones, usually have a hard time of it."

Sam looked down at her left wrist, at the horsehair bracelet that had become so much a part of her, she hardly saw it anymore.

The Phantom had been born in captivity. He'd been her horse from his birth and she hadn't set him free on purpose. An accident had done that.

She had that much in common with Diana, but there was one huge difference. Even as she lay in the hospital, she'd begged Dad to go after her horse. But Blackie couldn't be found, and it was pure luck that the tame colt had survived long enough to learn the lessons of the wild and become the Phantom.

Sam thought of the gentle chocolate mare. She'd make a great kids' horse, but not a mustang.

Wait. An idea bubbled around in Sam's mind. What if she used her college money to buy Lass, then sold her to Amelia's grandmother in place of Ace, and then put the money back in her savings account and gave the rest to Dad? Sam drummed her fingers on the table, watching each one touch down. What was wrong with the idea? Nothing that she could see. . . .

"Do you love Lass?" Gram asked.

"Of course I do," Diana said.

And there, Sam thought with a sigh, was the huge flaw in her idea.

"Then why didn't you stand up to the stable manager and tell him so, or talk with your father?" Gram asked.

Diana looked confused. "I felt kind of guilty, like, after all these years of neglecting her, what right did I have—"

"To save a faithful horse you love, and who obviously loves you back?" Brynna interrupted.

"Now you're going to make *me* cry," Kevin muttered.

"Can't you talk to your dad?" Sam asked. "I mean, it involves him."

Diana and Kevin looked at each other as if Diana's relationship with her father wasn't the best.

"It seems like the right thing to do," Sam added.

"It is," Diana said, "but that doesn't mean it's easy."

Gram filled the awkward moment by rising, finally, to get a plate of cookies.

"They're pecan pie bars," Gram said as she bustled back to the table. "If anyone's allergic to nuts—"

"No," Kevin and Diana said together as they saw the sweets.

"I guess you're all right," Brynna said. "If they released you from the hospital."

Diana nodded. "I think the final diagnosis was a tweaked shoulder, a bump on the head, and nausea due to stress."

Sam fidgeted in her chair. She should call Lynn and see if she wanted to talk with Diana, but she should also ask Diana if she wanted to talk with Lynn.

"Since you're going to keep her," Sam said, "would you mind talking with Lynn, the reporter you met yesterday? She's a friend of mine."

"I don't know," Diana said. "I'm not a huge fan of the media."

"They sensationalize stuff," Kevin added.

Sam took a breath. Lynn had done just the opposite. How could she convince these two of that? Then, she had an idea.

"So, I guess you saw the footage of Diana throwing up and being loaded into the ambulance yesterday," Sam said.

"What?" Kevin shouted. His mouth stayed open as he stared at Diana. "No!"

"Well, Lynn was there when it happened. And Lynn had film of the car accident, which would have tied in nicely with Diana getting checked and bandaged and—everything. But she didn't intrude. You didn't see that story because Lynn didn't sensationalize the accident."

Sam could see Diana weakening.

"And Lynn *did* do a story about a lost horse, even though she's scared to death of them," Sam said. "And if that horse had really, truly been lost, you might have found her because of it."

Sam was pretty happy with her argument, especially when Diana agreed.

After Sam's phone call, Lynn arrived and interviewed Diana gently. While the cameraman filmed Diana's joy at being reunited with her horse, Lynn took notes, learning facts about Rocky Mountain Horses that she'd share with her viewers.

"The breed just sprung up in the Appalachian Mountains," Diana said. "They're naturally gaited and suited for anything—hard travel, carrying kids, pulling plows, sleighs, and working cattle. Most of all, they're famous for their sweet temperaments," Diana said, and then she kissed Lass on the nose.

Before Lynn left, she pulled Sam aside. Sam could tell before the reporter said a word that she was going to bring up her accusations of Linc Slocum.

"So, he's not as bad as you thought, is he?" Lynn teased.

"He's even worse than I thought," Sam said stubbornly. "He's just not the villain this time."

Lynn laughed. "That's why a good journalist always looks for evidence."

"I guess," Sam said.

"It's disappointing," Lynn said as Sam walked her back to her news van. "But even criminals are innocent sometimes."

Lynn climbed into the van and started it, but before she drove away she lowered her window.

"Sam?" she called, smiling. "If he's really that crooked, there'll be a next time, and I'll be more than happy to be there."

Chapter Sixteen ❧

$\mathcal{L}$ ynn had left for the television studio. Kevin and Diana had loaded up Lass. They were planning to go talk to Diana's dad.

"We need to tell him we're getting married, too," Diana said. "That's going to blow him away. So, with any luck, he won't even notice I stole a horse!"

They'd left laughing, and now Sam stood brushing Ace.

This might be our last ride together, Sam thought.

She paused and touched her chest as if she could feel her heart breaking.

She kept brushing, but she couldn't stop thinking about her dream. It was as if it had tossed some kind of net over her.

A *gossamer net,* she thought, remembering that word from a vocabulary lesson in English. She was pretty sure the definition she'd found in the dictionary just said something like "delicate" or "flimsy," but to her, it had a mystical feel. All day she'd imagined the dream's invisible net surrounding her, even though it allowed her to eat and talk and do her chores.

Almost finished, Sam looked down at Ace's gleaming leg. There, where the bay darkened into glistening black, he was beautiful. And his hooves, so small that their imprint would fit her palm, were amazing. Hardened by years of galloping across the *playa,* up and down shale hillsides, they made him more sure-footed than any mountain goat. Would anyone in his new home appreciate his beauty, or would they just think of him as a plain, brown horse?

Sam saddled Ace, drawing the cinch and checking it twice.

"We'll have to tell them you're a tricky guy," Sam said, kissing the star on his forehead before she mounted up.

Sam was riding past the house when Gram stood up from her garden.

"I don't know why we keep that useless dog around," she snapped, using the back of her hand to wipe her forehead. "To think I was so worried over his night ramblings."

"What happened?" Sam asked.

"He's let the deer get in and eat all my strawberries," Gram said, "and then he dug himself a nice cool place to rest in my herb garden! My thyme and rosemary were just ready to harvest. I was giving them one more day." Gram stopped and shook her head.

"I'm sorry, Gram, I don't think he meant to destroy it," Sam said, turning Ace toward the bridge.

"When you get back, promise me you'll do something about the stack of phone messages you're accumulating," Gram said.

"I will," Sam said, and then she heard the phone ringing in the kitchen. Since there was no sense in putting off the call, Sam swung down from her saddle.

"I'll get it," she said, ground-tying Ace, and if Gram mumbled something after her, she didn't hear exactly what.

The kitchen was little cooler than the ranch yard, but Sam felt chilled as she crossed the room to pick up the telephone.

She was so braced to do the right thing, she almost didn't recognize Jake's voice.

"I've been thinking about Ace," he said, as if it was still yesterday morning and Sam had just told him about the offer.

"Oh, swell, you sure took your time about it."

"Good thoughts take a little longer," Jake said, and there was an irritability in his voice that made Sam wonder if he'd come in off the range just to call her. She couldn't take a chance that he'd hang up.

"Thanks," she said. "Go ahead and tell me what you figured out."

"I'm not makin' the decision for you, but, uh, are you sure Ace is the horse they want for that therapy job?"

Sam remembered Ace rearing at the fairgrounds. Ace panicking at the sound of the water truck and leading a rush for the far end of the pasture, just an hour ago, because he'd heard an unfamiliar noise.

"You aren't saying that just to make me happy, are you?" Sam asked.

"'Course not."

Sam sat in silence, waiting for Jake to convince her she wouldn't be selfish if she refused to sell Ace. When he finally spoke again, it sounded as if he'd started thinking about something else.

"You know when I was helping you with math last summer," Jake said.

"Don't remind me."

"Well, you think best with a pencil in your hand. You might write down the facts about that horse."

"Okay . . ."

"I gotta go," Jake said, and hung up.

When she heard dial tone, Sam hung up, too.

"What was *that*?" Sam lifted her hands toward the ceiling in a frustrated gesture, then realized she was talking to herself.

If Jake had called to help, he'd done a lousy job of it.

Sam paced back outside, jammed a boot in her stirrup, and swung into the saddle.

"It wasn't her. It was Jake," she said before Gram could ask.

"Those messages have been sitting on the kitchen table since yesterday," Gram went on, as if Sam hadn't said a word.

Sam gritted her teeth, but managed to be polite.

"I'll call as soon as I get back. I promise, Gram." Sam clucked Ace and rode on.

Sam's a good girl. She knows what's important. She'll do her part.

Gram and Dad's bragging about her to Hal didn't make her decision easier, just more obvious. As she rode across the bridge, heading for the range, there was Dad's truck, pushed off to the side.

Dead as a doornail, he'd said. He'd almost joked about it, too, as if he knew the money to fix or replace it would come from somewhere.

Fire danger was high and water was low, Sam thought as she rode Ace across the La Charla River. His hooves slipped on rocks that would have been submerged during a year with more rain.

Should she ride right, toward War Drum Flats, or left, toward the Phantom's territory? She loosened her hold on the reins, giving Ace his head, and he veered toward mustang country.

She'd just done what she'd told Diana not to do, Sam realized. You didn't let your horse choose its own path.

But I'm not going to strip off his saddle and bridle and let him decide whether he wants to rejoin the Phantom, Sam thought. She'd like to, but Ace was tame now. He knew where he could get food, water, and love, and he'd just come home.

Up ahead, wisps of smoke blew across the horizon.

She drew in her reins, but Ace strained against the bit and kept going.

"Whoa, boy," she told him. "Don't tell me you got used to being a brat at the rodeo, because I won't believe you. If that's smoke, the smart thing to do is go the other way."

Ace stopped, swung his head around, and stamped a front hoof.

"Good boy," Sam said, but she'd barely uttered the words when Ace's head swung around and he nipped the toe of her boot.

"Hey!" she shouted. "What are you thinking?"

Ace tossed his head skyward, eyes rolling, then he shook from nose to tail.

Now what? Sam thought. But then she saw what she'd missed.

Eight white horses marched in single file up the mustang path over the stair-step mesas. Sam blinked. Eight white horses?

She couldn't make sense of what she was seeing, until she recalled the way Ace had just shook.

The Phantom's herd was returning home from their dusting spot.

They'd rolled in the chalky dust of the *playa*. Though they looked like fairy-tale horses, they'd really been scratching itchy spots, rubbing off bugs, and loosening old hair so that their coats would gleam once the dust blew away.

Every few steps, a herd member stopped to shake, creating a white haze that swirled around them.

Judging from her muscled conformation, Sam was pretty sure the big honey-colored mare led the way, though she was a pale peach color in her dust coat.

Eight wild white horses, Sam thought. A white *playa*, and far off, the white-tipped peaks of the Calico Mountains.

Ace raised his head, testing the hot wind. At first, Sam was sure he'd scented the Phantom, but she didn't see the stallion.

Could that be him?

Sam loosed her reins and urged Ace closer to a fan of dust.

Stark white from alkali powder, the Phantom lay flat on his side. Tail outspread, head pressed to the *playa*, he rubbed his cheek back and forth against the hot desert floor. With eyes closed, he gave a groan of pleasure.

Then, hearing their approach or feeling the vibrations of Ace's hooves, the Phantom sensed he was no longer alone.

He rolled to his other side. So quickly his movements were blurred, his hind legs drew up against his belly, his forelegs extended to almost a sitting position, and he was up. Head lowered, eyes flashing a warning, the stallion stared their way.

"No dust bath for you today," Sam whispered to Ace. "I think he's just embarrassed to be caught off guard."

Ace was in no mood for jokes, and he backed up abruptly. Sam fought to keep her seat. In that instant, when Sam was making up her mind about Ace's future, the Phantom proved he was serious.

A mirage horse in the midst of a dust cloud, the stallion reared.

Mouth agape as he returned to all fours, he slashed the air with bright teeth before whirling, kicking, then rocketing after his mares.

Once he reached the second plateau, the Phantom stopped, stared back over his shoulder, and gave a snort.

Once Ace echoed the sound, the stallion turned and trotted away.

"That was good-bye," Sam whispered to Ace, and when she used her reins to signal a turn, Ace obeyed.

He didn't question a single command all the way home.

* * *

When Sam turned Ace out into the pasture, she wished she could roll in the cool grass with him.

It must be a hundred degrees, she thought, taking slow, dragging steps toward the house.

Gram stood on the porch, face shiny with perspiration, fanning herself with the skirt of her apron.

"Samantha."

Sam stopped. Just the stress on the middle syllable of her name told Sam that Gram was even crankier than she'd been over Blaze and the garden. Did she still have time to turn around and run for the barn? Cleaning stalls was more fun than facing Gram in hot weather.

But Gram had come down the steps to hold a slip of paper in front of Sam's face.

"I don't know why you're avoiding this woman, but here's another call."

Sighing, Sam took the message.

"It's a different number," Sam noticed.

"She said it was toll-free and you should call as soon as possible," Gram said. "Now I'm going upstairs to take a shower as soon as I finish cleaning this table."

Sam watched as Gram spread a square of flannel with lemon oil, then leaned her weight against her palm to polish the kitchen table.

Why would you do a chore like that on such a hot day?

I'm smart enough not to ask, Sam thought, although nothing could be worse than calling Amelia's grandmother and telling her she'd accept the three thousand dollars for Ace.

"Dinner's going to be late," Gram muttered as she buffed. "In fact, I don't feel much like cooking. If anyone wants more than sandwiches and chips, they can by golly bake it themselves."

The phone rang just as Sam was ready to lift the receiver.

"Hello?"

"Oh, Samantha, I've finally reached you."

The pleasant voice must belong to Amelia's grandmother. That surprised Sam. Because she hated the thought of selling her horse, she'd imagined the woman would sound like a witch.

"I'm afraid I have some bad news for you, dear."

Sam held the phone more tightly. Should she still sell Ace if Amelia's grandmother couldn't offer three thousand dollars?

No. She'd made her decision.

Ace was smart, but he was cow smart, not city smart, or riding ring smart. Ace was calm, but he was mustang calm, and that meant he could not ignore threats. Ace was patient, but—Sam shook her head and quit arguing with herself.

Three thousand dollars was a lot of money, but it wasn't worth the risk that Ace would harm a child.

I'm not being selfish, Sam thought, *I'm looking at the facts and being smart.*

"Bad news?" Sam said, and then she rushed to add, "Amelia's all right, isn't she?"

"What now?" Gram grumbled, but when Sam glanced over, she saw that Gram was staring at a light spot on the tabletop.

"Oh, yes, of course. Amelia's delighted to be riding again, and promising to be a model student in September, but it's about the therapy horse program and your Ace." She cleared her throat and Sam waited. "I saw those pictures of him acting up."

"Pictures?" Sam asked.

"Yes, you were wearing matching cowgirl outfits with a blond girl, and riding on each side of a bunch of cows."

For a minute Sam only remembered Lynn's cameraman shooting film for the six o'clock news, but then she recalled the whine of a camera's motor drive taking frame after frame of photographs.

"It was on the front page of the Denver paper, dear, and if anyone should find out that I'd donated a, well, *bucking bronco* as a therapy horse, what would they think?" She paused for a second, but when Sam didn't respond, she added, "Not to mention the safety of the children."

Could you feel let down and thankful at the same time?

Sam searched for words, but all she came up with

was, "It's okay. I understand."

"That's lovely of you, dear."

"Wait," Sam said, looking down at the note she was holding. "I want to say I'm sorry I didn't call you back sooner. I really meant to—"

"Don't give it another thought," she said.

"And I really appreciate you leaving this 800 number. I was just about to phone."

"Oh dear, I'm afraid there must be someone else after you as well!" she chuckled. "I didn't leave an 800 number."

Sam stared at the slip of paper. Who could it have been?

"Well, you sound a little—distracted, Samantha, so I'll talk with you later, shall I? Perhaps we can still work something out with another horse."

"That would be great," Sam said, with more enthusiasm than she'd felt during the entire conversation. "Thanks so much."

Sam hung up. She turned, ready to stay calm until she'd explained everything to Gram. But when she saw that Gram had already gone upstairs, Sam exploded.

"He's mine!" she shouted at Cougar as the cat started into the kitchen for food. Hungry or not, he was too afraid of his suddenly crazed mistress to do anything besides spin around and sprint for the stairs.

She had to hug Ace.

She had to tell her horse that contrary to everything

she'd ever told him, sometimes there was a reward for bad behavior!

Sam straight-armed the screen door and burst into the ranch yard. A late scratching hen fluttered clucking out of the way as Sam sprinted toward the pasture.

"Ace!" Sam yelled. "Ace! You're not going any-place, you wild bronco!"

She didn't care who heard or how silly she looked! It hadn't been their last ride together after all.

Grazing horses tossed up their heads and pricked their ears in her direction.

"Ace, you're staying, you bad boy!" she bellowed, and Strawberry's snort started a stampede away from the gate. As hooves retreated to the far end of the pasture, only Ace remained. Swishing his tail and tilting his head to one side, he regarded Sam as if he understood.

"Ace," Sam whispered as the mustang took three quiet steps to the gate and hung his head over so that she could kiss his nose. "Ace, I love you."

"What *is* all this?" Dad yelled, but Sam didn't turn. "Honey, are you crying?"

"What's wrong, Sam?" Brynna's voice was tender as her arm circled Sam's shoulders.

Sam swallowed hard, trying to hold back the flood of tears that threatened to follow the first few. When she looked up and saw Dad, the tears stopped.

"What happened to you?" she sniffed.

Dad was coated with mud. Even his face was black with it, except for the places he'd cleared around his eyes and mouth.

"Irrigation problems, but what's this about Ace staying? Where the heck did he think he was going to go?"

"I was going to sell him," Sam admitted. "I had an offer for three thousand dollars, exactly what you needed to deposit on a new truck, and—"

"And when were you going to talk to me about that?" Dad demanded.

It was hard to take him seriously because he was smeared in mud, but all at once Sam remembered telling Diana that she should talk to her father because he was involved in her decision. Taking her own advice had never occurred to her.

"It was going to be a surprise?" Sam asked, sniffing again.

"I don't think so," Dad said. As he gave his head a quick shake, a bit of mud splatted to the ground. "Ace is my horse and he's not for sale."

Brynna's arm left Sam's shoulder and she threw both her arms around Wyatt for a hug.

"You're crazy," Sam said, looking at the mess Brynna had made of her white blouse.

"Well, I'm hungry," Dad said, smiling as he strode toward the house. "And as soon as I clean up, I'm going to see what your Gram has for dinner."

"Uh, Gram's in the shower and she said it was too

hot to cook dinner," Sam said when they'd almost reached the porch.

Dad didn't have time to react before Gram called out.

"Samantha Anne Forster—"

Gram stood in the doorway, wearing a bath towel and a shower cap.

"Wyatt, Brynna," Gram said, spotting them. "The strangest thing has happened."

Dad and Brynna looked at each other as if they'd keep their opinions to themselves about strange things, but Gram kept talking.

"I'd just stepped into the shower and the telephone began ringing. It kept ringing and since it was clear no one else would answer it, I stormed down the stairs and who should it be but someone asking me if I was the legal guardian of Samantha Forster."

Sam flinched a little. What could that be about?

"And of course I thought, 'Lands, what has that child done now?' but I said 'yes.' And then she asked did I know Samantha had entered a contest at the rodeo. And I said it didn't surprise me, and then she started prattling on, telling me that if you win a vehicle you still had to pay tax and license because that wasn't included and—" Gram paused for a breath. "I'm afraid that was the stage at which I actually shouted at the poor dear to get to the point because I was making a huge puddle in the middle of my kitchen floor and well—Wyatt, Brynna, it seems that Samantha has won us a brand-new truck!"

"Yay!" Brynna shouted, then bulldogged Sam in a hug that smeared *her* with mud, too.

"Well, I'll be!" Dad said as a white grin showed through the mud on his face. "I say this calls for a celebration—of losin' three thousand dollars and winning the first new truck I've ever had in my whole life!"

As everyone cheered and made quick plans to drive to Clara's coffee shop for a celebratory dinner, Sam couldn't resist a detour back to the pasture. She had to give Ace one last hug.

Her arms were wrapped around his warm brown neck when Dad appeared beside her.

"Honey," he said, "that money mighta helped out, and the truck certainly will, but no matter what happens, that horse is yours for the rest of his life, and I'll hear no argument about it. Ever."

And Sam said, "Okay."

From

Phantom Stallion

⌒ 18 ⌒

FIREFLY

$\mathcal{S}$amantha Forster dug her fingers past the crust of garden soil, cooked hot by the August sun. She felt the cool dirt at the base of a plant. Was it a weed?

Gram had assigned her to clear the vegetable garden of weeds, hinting that early morning was a good time to get started.

In shorts and a tank top instead of her usual boots and jeans, Sam worked in the shade of her white house, headquarters of River Bend Ranch.

Sam had awakened thinking of the river walk she'd take this morning with her foal Tempest. Her dreams had been filled with the splashing of tiny black hooves in the La Charla River shallows.

Sam hummed along with songs floating from the

radio Gram had left on the porch. She felt cooler just picturing the wading horses, until the disc jockey broke into her daydream.

"If you're within the sound of my voice brace yourself for the hottest week of the year. We're looking at a record 106 degrees by midweek and I call that a scorcher—hot enough to fry an egg on the sidewalk, I'll betcha!"

Sam wiped her forehead with the back of one dirty hand.

"Only someone sitting in an air-conditioned studio could sound so cheerful," she grumbled to Blaze, who lay beside her as she knelt in Gram's garden.

The Border collie raised his head from between his paws, panted in agreement, then returned to his doze.

Snorts and squeals, the clacking of teeth and thump of hooves came from the ten-acre pasture. The saddle horses felt the high desert heat gathering. For several days, most of them had stood under the cottonwood tree at the far end of the enclosure. Now, their pent-up energy erupted in crankiness.

Shading her eyes, Sam searched the pasture for Popcorn.

The albino gelding stood apart from the others. His white tail swished at flies as he watched Penny, another captive mustang, enjoy pats and coddling from Brynna, Sam's stepmother.

Would the soaring temperatures affect Popcorn's usual calm with this week's H.A.R.P. girls? The Horse and Rider Protection program brought at-risk girls together with captive mustangs. Though Sam thought it was a great program and believed River Bend Ranch was lucky to be part of it, the girls could be—how had Brynna put it?—oh yeah, a challenge.

A porch board squeaked and Sam looked up to see Gram fanning herself with the hem of her red apron.

On hot days like this, Gram began cooking in predawn darkness so she didn't have to turn on the oven later. As Sam rolled out of bed this morning, the aromas of fresh bread, brownies, cheddar cheese, and chili peppers had wafted up the stairs.

Flushed but satisfied, Gram said, "Baking's finished and the chili con queso is just simmering in the Crock-Pot. I'm about done for the—Samantha, no!"

Sam snatched her hand back from the dirt and scrambled to her feet. What had Gram seen? A snake, scorpion, spider?

"That's better," Gram said. "If you hadn't loosened your death grip on my morning glory vine, you would have uprooted it, instead of that weed," Gram said.

"Sorry," Sam apologized. She was almost sorry a venomous pest hadn't been skulking around her fingertips. She probably could have left off weeding for the day.

"The point is to pull out the weeds that are gulping up the precious little water we can give them," Gram explained.

"Okay," Sam said, though the explanation didn't help much. To her, weeds and flowers looked a lot alike.

Green and spindly, they crawled over the dirt, then slung slender tendrils around the wire trellis Gram had put up. Higher up, the morning glories bloomed with blue, trumpet-shaped flowers, but when they were getting started, they looked just like the weeds.

"I know they all look alike at first," Gram said. "You have to learn to tell the difference. Water's precious. I save it for the tomatoes and green beans, corn and strawberries, because we can eat them."

"What about the roses?" Sam asked. She'd been thinking they were purely ornamental, but as soon as the words were out, she thought of Gram's rose-hip tea.

"The roses are something of a luxury," Gram admitted. "Though my rose-hip tea is full of vitamin C, and the quickest way to cure a cold." She looked at the trellis almost tenderly. "But the morning glories don't ask for much and they keep showing up on their own. Seems like the least we can do is clear away the weeds."

Sam nodded, but she still didn't really get it. Her only hope was to memorize the ones Gram pointed out as weeds.

Cackling and squawking, three Rhode Island Red hens flapped up a dust cloud nearby. Sam thought they were squabbling over the cracked corn she'd scattered for them earlier, until she heard Brynna's voice.

"You feel up to seeing the mustang colt from the Deerpath fire?"

Sam glanced up as Brynna walked toward her. With her hair pulled back in its usual red braid, and a sleeveless white blouse hanging loose over jeans, she looked more like a teenager than the manager of a government agency.

Brynna had been the boss at Willow Springs Wild Horse Center for three years. She acted as guardian and overseer of the wild horses which roamed the thousands of acres surrounding River Bend Ranch.

Brynna didn't look like anyone's pregnant step-mother, either, Sam thought, but she was that, too.

"What do you mean, 'feel up to it'?" Sam asked, flipping back the auburn bangs which were already stuck to her forehead with sweat.

"He got some pretty nasty burns," Brynna said carefully.

Instantly Sam thought of the Phantom, and her stomach dipped.

Two horses had been hurt the day that lightning sparked a fire, which had blackened twenty acres of ranch land and heated the cans of paint sitting next to Mrs. Allen's fence to the point of exploding.

Sam had been following Mrs. Allen's directions, but she'd been the one who'd left those cans there. She still felt guilty for the horses' injuries.

The Phantom, a graceful silver stallion which had once been hers, had been temporarily deafened by the concussion of the exploding paint cans. He'd been burned, too, and the scorched place on his neck had turned shriveled and dark. It had looked exactly like a burned marshmallow.

The Phantom had been injured as he'd raced after a youngster from his herd. He'd tried to herd the yearling out of danger, but he'd been too late.

The yearling had suffered burns all over his face.

Sam winced in sympathy for the young horse, but she'd seen injured animals before. Of course she was up to seeing the colt. She owed it to him and because of Brynna, she might even have a chance to help him.

As the federal government's local representative in charge of the wild horses' welfare, Brynna had authorized expensive veterinary care for the colt.

"The last time we saw him," Sam said, "his face was mainly swollen from smoke inhalation. That's got to have gone down by now, and probably, that made him look worse."

"I'm sure," Brynna said. "But —" Brynna stopped speaking.

As Brynna broke off, Sam recognized the look in her stepmother's eyes. Most of the time, especially when it came to horses, Brynna treated Sam as an adult. Brynna was a biologist, and though she loved animals, she wasn't sentimental about them. She usually told the truth straight out.

"There's no point trying to fool yourself, Sam. His burned nose and the damage to that white patch around his eye has changed his appearance."

"I know," Sam said and her memory brought back the time she'd spent crouched beside the colt.

A black crust had replaced the tender skin on the colt's nose. The patch of white hair around one eye had burned away, leaving behind skin that looked scarlet with sunburn. But damage done by flames wouldn't fade like sunburn.

Poor Pirate.

She'd never used the nickname aloud, but the bay colt's swaggering boldness, paired with his unusual white marking had made her call him Pirate.

She'd seen him for the first time on Dad and Brynna's wedding day, the morning he'd caused the Phantom's herd to nearly trample her. Still, it hadn't been his fault, and Sam had always liked the rowdy bay colt.

It hadn't been hard persuading Brynna and Dr. Scott, the young vet on retainer to the Bureau of Land Management, to rescue the colt. The last time Sam had talked with Dr. Scott, though, he'd been worried over the colt's future.

"Are you putting him up for adoption?" Sam asked.

"Not yet. Dr. Scott wants to foster him out."

Perfect, Sam thought. That way the colt could get the loving care he needed.

Sam bolted to her feet and her gaze took in the ranch yard.

Where could they put an injured yearling?

Read all the Phantom Stallion Books!

#1: The Wild One
Pb 0-06-441085-4

#2: Mustang Moon
Pb 0-06-441086-2

#3: Dark Sunshine
Pb 0-06-441087-0

#4: The Renegade
Pb 0-06-441088-9

#5: Free Again
Pb 0-06-441089-7

#6: The Challenger
Pb 0-06-441090-0

#7: Desert Dancer
Pb 0-06-053725-6

www.phantomstallion.com

#8: Golden Ghost
Pb 0-06-053726-4

#9: Gift Horse
Pb 0-06-056157-2

#10: Red Feather Filly
Pb 0-06-056158-0

#11: Untamed
Pb 0-06-056159-9

#12: Rain Dance
Pb 0-06-058313-4

#13: Heartbreak Bronco
Pb 0-06-058314-2

#14: Moonrise
Pb 0-06-058315-0

#15: Kidnapped Colt
Pb 0-06-058316-9

#16: The Wildest Heart
Pb 0-06-058317-7

AVON BOOKS

An Imprint of HarperCollinsPublishers